SEVEN DAYS

ANDREW GREY

Dreamspinner Press

Published by
Dreamspinner Press
4760 Preston Road
Suite 244-149
Frisco, TX 75034
http://www.dreamspinnerpress.com/

Seven Days

Cover Art by Justin James   dare.empire@gmail.com
Cover Design by Mara McKennen

ISBN: 978-1-61581-879-2

Printed in the United States of America
First Edition
April 2011

eBook edition available
eBook ISBN: 978-1-61581-880-8

Readers love Andrew Grey

A Taste of Love

"…an emotional story that will have you in tears one minute, smiling and laughing the next."
—Love Romances & More

A Shared Range

"…another enjoyable read filled with two well rounded and likable guys."
—Literary Nymphs

Pump Me Up

"Andrew Grey is a master storyteller. His stories have heart and the characters fairly leap off the pages to completely captivate you."
—Love Romances & More

An Unexpected Vintage

"There's nothing like a story that reminds you to get out and enjoy life!"
—Fallen Angel Reviews

Love Means… Freedom

"Mr. Grey has, once again, brought to life compelling characters with whom readers can identify and about whom we can care deeply. This is one of those books best read snuggled up in a cozy, favorite chair while the wind howls outside."
—Whipped Cream Erotic Romance Reviews

http://www.dreamspinnerpress.com

Books by
ANDREW GREY

Accompanied by a Waltz
A Taste of Love
Seven Days

THE BOTTLED UP STORIES
Bottled Up
Uncorked
The Best Revenge
An Unexpected Vintage

THE RANGE STORIES
A Shared Range
A Troubled Range

THE CHILDREN OF BACCHUS STORIES
Children of Bacchus
Thursday's Child
Child of Joy

THE LOVE MEANS… STORIES
Love Means… No Shame
Love Means… Courage
Love Means… No Boundaries
Love Means… Freedom
Love Means … No Fear

All published by
DREAMSPINNER PRESS

This story is dedicated to Dominic. His willingness and courage to share details of his high school years made this story possible.

Chapter 1

EVAN stepped out of the warm car with its leather seats, vents blasting warm air and clean scent. He thought of looking back at the man driving, but he didn't really matter. Evan knew that—at least he did now. Stepping out onto the sidewalk, nearly slipping on the slushy snow, he closed the door and jumped back as the dark blue Mercedes sped away in a fountain of water, dirt, and half-melted slush. Looking around to get his bearings in the early morning gloom, he backed farther away from the street, running into someone who simply shoved him away with a grunt. With another stumble, he reached the brick building, leaning against it, taking stock of what he had and where he was, hands sliding instinctively into his pockets as they sought some sort of warmth. The hardest thing to get used to and get his mind around was the near-constant cold.

His hands slid along the folded bills, and Evan breathed a sigh of relief. Those small slips of paper, vital for everything on the streets, were a lifeline to a warm night and maybe even a bath or shower to wash away the scents of others on his body. Pulling out the bills, he slipped off a tattered shoe. Rolling down a sock, he shoved the bills deep under his arch with the others before rolling the sock up again. The sound of ripping fabric made him groan, and he looked down as the top of the sock, a few inches above his ankle, came away in his hand. Sliding his shoe back on, he left the tattered piece of fabric just above his ankle for warmth, letting his pant leg slide back down. His money hidden, Evan relaxed a little, looking around for that signal, the look that would indicate another man who might be willing to pay for what he was selling. Pulling his thin jacket around his body, Evan huddled against the building, his skin prickling, legs beginning to shake, arms aching as the cold seeped in through the jacket and his thin shirt.

Watching passersby, he caught the eye of a man in a business suit and long woolen coat sauntering down the street like he owned the world, and to Evan it looked like he did. The man, who might have been on his way to work, passed and continued walking before stopping, looking through the glass of a shop window. Evan knew he wasn't really looking into the shop. That was one of the traits he'd already picked up on. No one ever approached him right away; the men were usually shy or cautious. Evan watched as the man turned and walked back toward him, stopping just a few feet away without looking directly at him. "Sure is cold," the man said, looking around the street.

"Yup," Evan replied, trying to stay out of the wind.

"Bet it's warmer between the buildings," the man commented, a not-so-subtle hint at what he wanted.

Warily, Evan pushed himself away from the building, taking a few steps and looking around before following the man's line of sight, saying nothing more. He heard the man's footsteps behind him and braced himself. He hated this, he really did. A few months ago, he'd been a normal kid with normal parents and a normal life, and thoughts of what he was about to do had never entered his mind. Now it was an almost daily occurrence just to eat and maybe have a warm place to sleep. "Fifty," Evan said and waited to see what the guy would do.

"You've got to be kidding," the man said, and Evan moved back toward the street. He already had some money, and with it, he knew he'd eat. The man's hands slipped into his pocket, pulling out crumpled bills. Evan took them, shoving the bills deep into his own pocket. The man pushed down on his shoulders, and Evan felt his knees buckle, pain shooting through his legs as his knees hit the slush-covered pavement, even more cold seeping into his skin. The teeth of a zipper sounded, and Evan began to retreat, his conscious mind pulling away, sheltering himself from the implications of what was about to happen—it was the only thing that stopped him from gagging, stopped the reflex to bite, to get away, or even to hurt. The only way he could bear the man's voice as he called Evan every disgusting name in the book. Evan heard these, though; they penetrated his defenses because he'd said them to himself. He knew they were true because, after all, he was a "dirty fucking whore."

Tears welled, as they always did, and he blinked them back as the man's calls became more urgent. Pulling away, he could take no more. Jumping to his feet, legs wet, prickling with cold, Evan forced himself to move as the man howled his frustration. Evan peeked back and saw him pumping himself as Evan turned the corner, heart pounding. Realizing he wasn't being chased, he slowed and stopped in front of a bright department store window, puddles of water glistening with reflected light. Evan looked down, and catching a glimpse of his own reflection, he actually looked over his shoulder wondering if someone was behind him. He took a second look and realization dawned: the thin, drawn, old-looking face staring back at him was him.

Stepping away, out of the light, Evan huddled beneath the awning of a dark window. His knees aching, he slid down the marble-tiled wall. Arms encircling his knees, body curling into a tight ball, forehead resting on his knees, Evan felt the tears that had threatened multiple times come to the surface. "Mom... Dad... why'd you leave me?" he asked for what seemed like the millionth time as his throat tightened. Shoulders bouncing, Evan couldn't stop the emotions that he'd held at bay for months. As they burst to the surface, he murmured, "I miss you both," and he felt his face contort into the near-universal display of grief. He could see them saying goodbye that last Saturday morning as they'd left the house to go shopping. He'd asked to stay home, and as the tears ran down his cheeks, Evan wished with all his might that he'd gone with them. That way, the semitrailer that had skidded on the ice, crushing his parents' lives and his entire world, could have taken him too.

"Son." A hand touched his shoulder, and Evan jumped up, bouncing on his feet, arms bent, hands already clenched in tight fists. The man simply looked at him, his face calm, hands remaining at his side. "I'm not going to hurt you," he said levelly, almost serenely.

Evan felt his arms become heavy and he lowered them, his body ready to run at the slightest provocation. "What is it you want?" Evan asked, taking a step back, hitting the wall behind him. "I'm not interested in any customers, so you can just move on." Evan looked the man over, starting at the clean, plain shoes, black pants and plain coat, open to show just the edge of a black shirt with a bit of white collar. "Oh," he said softly, "one of those." He'd had ministers and priests before, and at least they'd been gentler than most, even as they used him like everyone else. "Fifty," he said softly and moved toward the darkness around the side of the store as the streets began to fill.

"No, son," the man responded gently, "that's not what I want." Evan felt the fight seep away, and he turned to move on. If the man wasn't a customer, Evan had money, and he could find a warm place for the day and maybe get some sleep and fill his empty and howling belly. "I can help you," the man called after Evan, without yelling, a softness in his voice that Evan hadn't heard from anyone since…. Evan blinked and shoved his hurt and pain back behind the walls his mind was rapidly reconstructing after the earlier breach. "I don't want anything from you," the priest added. "I promise. Can I buy you some breakfast?" He motioned toward a small diner just across the street. "I promise I won't hurt you."

Evan watched as the priest—he assumed he was a priest, but he could have been any kind of minister as far as Evan knew—walked across the street, looking back at him before opening the door to the diner and disappearing inside. His mind struggled, trying to decide what to do, but in the end it was his growling stomach that made up his mind for him, and he stepped off the curb, a taxi blowing its horn at him. Evan let it pass, giving the driver both fingers, because that's just what you did to cabbies, before feeling the fight and the last remaining energy in his body begin to slip away. Walking the rest of the way across the street, he stopped at the glass before reaching out to pull open the door.

Evan caught the sneer on the face of the woman behind the counter. What he'd ever done to her he didn't know, but he'd always avoided this place because of her and the sneer she always gave him, like he was something she'd scrape off her shoe, and maybe that's what he was. Maybe he was no better than the dirt off her shoes.

Looking around, he spied the priest sitting at a table, watching him. Seeing him nod slightly, Evan slowly walked in his direction, watching his reaction. "Sit down. It's okay," the priest said, and Evan slipped into the booth, sliding across from the other man, looking for any sign of deceit or subterfuge, but the man's expression seemed as open and honest as he could remember since he found himself on the streets. There had to be something this man wanted from him—no one did something for nothing. That he'd found out fast when the man who'd helped him the first night he found himself alone tried to take what it was he wanted. Evan had learned fast, and quickly became wary of anyone and everyone.

A waitress, old as the hills, approached their table, smiling at the priest but scowling at him. She handed the priest a menu before grudgingly setting one in front of Evan and leaving. "What do you want?" Evan asked, his eyes boring into the other man, challenging him to try to lie to him.

The waitress returned, and the priest placed an order for a huge breakfast, and Evan said he'd have the same, figuring he might as well eat if nothing else.

"What's your name, son?" the priest asked, and he waited as the waitress brought cups of coffee. Evan wrapped his hands around his, letting the warmth thaw his nearly numb hands.

"What do you want it to be?" Evan asked, a cliché answer, but he never told anyone his real name. It felt to him that if he did, he'd be giving up that last bit of himself, that last remnant of who he was before everything changed.

"Don't play games. I will not stand for that," the man admonished firmly, but with a tone completely absent of malice.

Evan swallowed hard, taking a sip of the coffee, heat sliding down his throat and settling in his belly. Setting down the mug, he reached for the sugar packets, ripping open about four, dumping them into the black liquid before drinking again. The priest said nothing more, but stern, brown eyes tinged with kindness stared back at him.

"Evan," he finally said, in a near whisper.

"Good. I'm Father Valentin, and as I said before, I will not hurt you in any way," the priest said as he sipped the coffee, making a face before setting the mug back on the table. "Can you tell me how old you are?"

"Of course, you think I'm dumb or something?" Evan retorted. "I'm sixteen and I can take care of myself." Evan again dared the priest with his eyes to contradict him.

"I'm sure you can," he responded with a smile. The waitress returned and placed a plate in front of each of them. Evan picked up a piece of toast, shoving the entire thing into his mouth, chewing and swallowing before devouring the other. Lifting his fork, he attacked the eggs before downing the slippery potatoes in three bites. "I promise you, no one will take your plate from you," the man teased.

Evan ignored him, shoveling in the food as fast as he could swallow it, arm on the table protecting his turf as he scanned the immediate vicinity. Only when the plate was empty did he look up again to see the priest sort of smiling at him. "Thanks," Evan said softly, not knowing what else to say, as some long-forgotten voice whispered inside him what to do. The voice sounded a lot like his mother.

"Are you still hungry?" The priest didn't wait for an answer, taking Evan's plate and sliding his own in front of him. Evan felt his eyes widen and then began to eat again until his stomach felt truly full—a sensation he hadn't experienced since he'd discovered the fruit trees in the park last summer and had eaten his fill right from the tree, that is, until he was chased away.

"Evan, do you know where your parents are?"

He nodded but couldn't bring himself to say the words out loud. The thought felt like saying goodbye to them all over again. For months he'd kept hoping it was all a mistake, but it wasn't. And he knew it now, but he still couldn't say it, not to a stranger, anyway. Evan's expression seemed to be enough for the priest, because the man simply nodded.

"Evan, I can help you if you'll let me. I run a school for boys, and I'd like to take you there."

Evan got it now. The priest would take him to this "school" and in return for a place to sleep, Evan would take care of the priest. He'd heard about places like this from one of the other boys he'd met during the summer. Tom had been offered something like that by an old geezer who hung around the park. Last time he'd seen him, Tom was living it up, and all he had to do was let the geezer fuck him once in a while. "What do I have to do?" Evan leaned across the table, eyes locked on the priest's. "You want me to suck your dick—is that it?"

"No, Evan, I most certainly do not. I don't want anything from you except the truth when I ask a question. My order of priests and brothers are educators," he continued, "and we believe that every boy should have an education and a chance at a better life. At the school, you'll have duties that you'll need to perform, and there will be things we all expect from you, such as good behavior, completing your lessons, and showing respect to your instructors and fellow students."

"Nice speech, Father, but what is it you really want?"

"To give you a chance to get off the streets, to have a place that's safe and warm with plenty of food and no need for you to sleep in alleys or sell yourself for money."

Evan looked around at all the other patrons in the diner, trying to figure out if this guy was for real. He wanted to ask someone, but no one else even looked at them. "What are you, Santa Claus? 'Cause I stopped believing in that shit a long time ago."

"No, and I assure you what I'm offering you is for real. I believe that we must help our fellow man, and I want to help you. Will you let me?" the priest asked, before adding, "and don't swear to me or anyone else. That's another of our rules, and part of respecting others."

Was this man for real? Evan stared, trying to figure it out as the waitress brought the check, and Father Valentin picked it up, handing some cash to the waitress before standing. This seemed way too good to be true, but something inside him said he'd be a fool not to go along with it. If Father Valentin turned out to be as full of shit as he thought he was, he could always leave.

"Are you coming or not?" the priest asked, and Evan slid out of the booth, following behind, his hands once again sliding into his pockets, hands feeling the soiled bills like a security blanket. Outside, Father Valentin walked to where an old, clunky station wagon with fake wood trim was parked, and unlocked the door, holding it open for him and waiting. Evan got into the vehicle, wondering what he was so afraid of. He'd gotten into strange cars before, and not with men who said they wanted to help him. Maybe it was the wondering? When he'd gotten into cars before, he knew why he was doing it and what was expected, but now, he had no idea about any of it. Evan found himself watching as Father Valentin opened the driver's door and got into the car, starting the old engine with prayer and a few cajoling words. "Fasten your seatbelt. Bernadette here keeps running, but sometimes she's a little unpredictable." Father Valentin put the car into gear, and Evan felt a lurch as the car seemed to jump out into traffic.

They rode for a while through the traffic of the city and out into what looked to Evan to be a very old portion of Milwaukee. Beautiful homes shared space with what looked like dilapidated wrecks, except most of them were covered in scaffolding. Not thinking about it, Evan watched the road, memorizing landmarks in case he needed to leave and find his way back. He refused to let himself believe that anyone was willing to help him, but part of him, deep down, hoped that maybe, just maybe, Father Valentin was for real.

Many landmarks passed, and Evan tried to remember them, but then gave up. He knew he could survive, he'd done it for months, and he could and would do it again once he found out just what Father Valentin wanted from him. The old car bounced and pitched them over the patched roads. The buildings became lower, apartments replaced with homes, and then the ride got smoother as the houses got grander, and still they drove. The homes gave way to fields with barns, and animals Evan had never seen before, grazing and wandering.

A hill loomed on the horizon with a large building sitting on top of it, getting bigger and bigger as they approached. "That's the school," Father Valentin said, his hand pointing over the top of the steering wheel. Evan craned his head out the window as the building continued to climb over them. Evan thought it looked like some sort of haunted house, with its large windows and towers that loomed over the landscape. Shuddering slightly, he looked over at the driver, expecting him to have transformed into some sort of evil creature, but Father Valentin turned and smiled back at him. "I hope you like it here. This is a good place, and you'll be taken care of, I promise. Part of what we do is help those who need us, and when I saw you come out of that alley, I knew I had to try to help."

Evan looked at the floor, his feet shifting in his tattered shoes. He had no idea why Father Valentin seeing him in the alley bothered him, but it did. The man had been kind to him, so far, and while Evan refused to lower his guard, something inside him lifted. Was it hope? Evan wasn't sure and he actually tamped it down. Every time he'd felt that over the last months, he'd been let down again.

The car turned onto a long driveway lined with trees and began to climb, the road turning first one way and then the other until Father Valentin pulled into a parking lot. Evan kept trying to see the building, but it rose above them high enough that all he could see was mustard walls and a few brown window frames. "What is this?" Evan asked softly as he peered out and saw what looked like a church among the other buildings, all sitting on the top of the hill.

"This is St. Bartholomew's Academy for Boys," Father Valentin said proudly as he opened his door and climbed out of the car. Evan did the same, standing in the clean air, instantly cold again after the long drive in the warm car.

"Father, you're back."

Evan saw another man approach, bundled against the cold. "How was the conference with the bishop?"

"Fruitful, Brother William," he said before adding, "the car will need to be unloaded. Could you please see to it while I get Evan here inside and warmed up?"

"I... I... can help," Evan offered, his teeth chattering.

"Don't be silly, you're freezing." Father Valentin started toward a set of doors, and Evan followed, not having any idea what else to do. Going inside was like passing into another world, with warmth surrounding him almost instantly. "My office is this way," he said, gesturing, and Evan nodded slowly, following down the quiet hallway. "The other boys are in classes right now, but it'll get quite noisy soon," Father Valentin explained as they approached a large door. Pulling it open, Father Valentin motioned for him to enter, and Evan stepped forward, peering inside before looking back down the hall.

Part of him wanted to run. He'd already seen one statue of a man holding his own head and one of a man shot through with a bunch of arrows, and he wondered what kind of people spent time in a place like that. Looking into what appeared to be an office, Evan saw another statue, this one of a pretty lady with a blue cloak, and she looked nice, almost serene. Looking up at Father Valentin's face, he saw him smile and nod. Stepping inside, Evan looked around as Father Valentin stepped in behind him, closing the door. So this was when he'd get it? Evan thought as he watched the priest step around to his desk. "Sit down, Evan," Father Valentin said gently, motioning toward one of the chairs. "I have some questions for you, and I want you to answer them honestly. That's all we can ever ask of anyone, to be truthful. I promise not to judge or condemn you for your answers. Do you understand?"

Evan didn't, but he nodded his head anyway, hoping Father Valentin would get to whatever it was he wanted from him.

Father Valentin got up from behind the desk and walked around it before sitting in the chair next to his. "I know you're finding all this hard to believe, so I want to take a few minutes to explain things so you know what I'm offering you and what's expected of you." Father Valentin's voice sounded so kind and caring that, for the first time, Evan began to allow himself to believe that this might just be real. "This is a religious school," he continued to explain. "We'll test you to determine where you are academically and develop an appropriate schedule of classes. You'll attend mass every day with all the other boys. In short, this school will be your home, and I, along with the other brothers, will be your family."

Evan lifted his eyes from the small stain on the carpet where he'd been staring. "What's the price? No one does anything for free, I know that. What is it you want?"

Father Valentin nodded slowly, his eyes remaining soft and kind. "The price is your education. All I ask is that you do your best in school to learn and to be a good, caring person. I neither expect nor want anything more from you. There are some rules that we follow here. One of them is respect for your teachers and fellow students. Another is that the type of behavior you engaged in prior to coming here is not tolerated." Father Valentin's voice became firm. "I understand you were trying to survive, and I can respect that, but here, we strive to lead lives pleasing to God, and that type of behavior is not acceptable." Evan could feel Father Valentin's eyes rake over him as though drilling the message into him. "What we will strive to provide for you is a safe place where you can learn to be a good young man and build a future for yourself beyond the streets."

Evan swallowed. *Was this for real? This truly was too good to be true.* "You really don't want anything from me?"

Father Valentin shook his head slowly. "No. Well, not in the way you're thinking. I do want things from you. I want you to be a good student and grow into a good man with a bright, promising future. Nothing more." He held up a finger, and Evan braced for the rug to be pulled away. "But I would like some answers."

"What kind of answers?" Evan asked tentatively.

"Let's start with your full name." Father Valentin picked up a pad of paper.

"Evan Donaldson," he answered, saying the full name out loud for the first time since his parents' death.

Father Valentin wrote for a second and then leaned forward in the chair, a quiet, serene expression on his face. "What happened to your family?" Evan knew at some point he'd have to talk about this, but he really had no desire to and shook his head before looking away. "I'm asking you to trust me, Evan. I will do nothing to hurt you, but I need to know what happened to you so I can try to help you."

"They died in an accident last spring," he answered to the floor. "I wish I'd been with them," Evan added as he swallowed hard, keeping a tenuous hold on the last of his emotional control.

"Was there no other family?" he heard Father Valentin ask, and Evan shook his head, not trusting himself to answer. "Were you sent to a foster home?" he asked softly, and Evan nodded. "Did they hurt you?" Evan shook his head, completely unable to explain that the foster parents were probably good people, but they weren't his parents, so in his mind, they were the worst people on earth.

"I left. They didn't want me anyway." That was the easiest explanation that fit the way Evan thought. He wasn't their child, and they weren't his parents, so they couldn't want him, and he certainly didn't want them. Evan lifted his eyes from the carpet and saw Father Valentin looking at him nervously. "I'm not going back there," he added before returning his gaze to the floor.

"I won't send you back. But do you remember when I said you had to be truthful? That goes both ways." Evan listened, wondering where this was going. "I need to call the authorities and tell them where you are. I can arrange for legal guardianship to be transferred to me, but I'll only do that if you allow me to."

Evan snapped his eyes to Father Valentin. "You're giving me a choice? That social worker bitch never did. She just dumped me with strangers!" It surprised Evan to realize he didn't consider Father Valentin a stranger. He didn't know what he considered him yet, not really, but he thought he could maybe trust him, sort of.

"Yes, you have a choice," Father Valentin said, reaching across the distance between them, touching his shoulder. "One of our other rules is that swearing of any kind is an offense to God," Father Valentin said flatly. "The social worker may have been a 'bitch', but we don't say it that way." Evan saw Father Valentin wink at him, and Father Valentin's lips turned up in what might have approximated a smile.

"Okay." He thought for a second. "How about witch with a capital B?" That's what his mother used to say. Evan choked around the lump that threatened in his throat.

Father Valentin smiled. "If you insist." Evan saw the smile fade. "How long ago did you leave the foster home?" Evan shrugged. It had been warm when he left, and the first few months had been easier, at least with finding a place to sleep.

"Spring, I guess," Evan answered, trying to remember. It seemed so long ago. With every day a fight for survival, time had little reference other than temperature and the weather. A soft knock on the door interrupted them, and Evan sank back into the chair as Father Valentin called for whoever it was to enter.

"I'm sorry to bother you, Father, but it's almost time for mass and…."

Father Valentin rose from his chair, and Evan heard his knees pop. "Thank you, Brother, you were quite right to remind me." The door closed again. "We should get ready. Come, I'll show you the way." Father Valentin walked to the office door and opened it, leading him down the now-noisy hallway filled with boys ranging from a few years younger to a few years older than he was. Evan kept his eyes cast down, careful not to meet anyone's gaze and still keep Father Valentin in sight. "The chapel is right over there. I need to change. Just go right inside and sit down."

Father Valentin hurried away, and Evan went where he'd pointed, going into the building and then through another set of doors to a large room with a soaring ceiling. He and his parents hadn't been to church much, but something about this room seemed to reach deep inside him. Turning to one side, Evan found a back corner, near one of the pillars, and sat down, his eyes darting all around before his head craned upward toward a painted ceiling. He'd never seen anything so beautiful, and his mouth sort of hung open as he stared.

The doors opening and the sound of overlapping voices brought him back, his gaze transferring itself to the floor. The boys all found places to sit, and their voices quieted. Slowly, Evan lifted his eyes and saw Father Valentin walk out, raising his hands, and everyone stood. Father Valentin began singing things, and then everyone sang back. Evan really couldn't make out many of the words, but he did his best to listen.

The back door of the church opened, and a single boy entered, peering around before closing the door quietly and sliding down to sit next to him. All the boys wore gray pants, white shirts, and blue jackets. The boy next to him touched his arm and handed him one of the blue jackets, motioning for him to put it on. Evan did, looking back at the other boy, wondering what was going on. He tried to mouth his question, but the dark-haired boy simply smiled at him before turning his attention back to the service.

Evan listened to what was happening around him, trying to pay attention, but his eyes kept wandering to the boy sitting next to him on the long hard wooden seat. Evan didn't know his name, but he did know he had sparkly brown eyes and an open face that made

Evan's insides feel funny when he'd smiled at him. He adjusted himself in his pants slightly and pulled the jacket closed around him. Not only did it keep him warmer, but it also hid other things he didn't want his companion to see. All through the service, he kept an eye on the boy with jet-black hair. "Amen," rang through the voluminous space as everyone sang in unison. Then quiet descended for half a second until everyone began to talk again, all the boys heading at once toward the exit.

Evan tried to follow the boy, walking between the wooden seats, but he seemed to join the others and got almost carried away. Not knowing where to go, Evan stopped and stayed where he was until he saw Father Valentin walking toward him. "Good, I see you got a jacket. Excellent," he said, stopping. "I think we need to get you some lunch. Then you can clean up, and we'll find you a room."

Evan nodded and followed, wondering for the millionth time what he was doing here and why this man in particular was being so kind to him. Father Valentin led him back to his office, where he had one of the brothers bring them both some lunch, and then Evan found himself led to a small, private bathroom. "I'll have some uniforms brought for you, and I'll see what I can do to find you clothes to wear on the weekends."

Evan turned back. "I can't pay for all of this," he said softly, reaching into his pockets, hands sliding over the bills for a second before he pulled them out and handed them to Father Valentin without saying anything. Before he closed the bathroom door, Evan saw the priest's eyes widen, and then his mouth curled into a smile.

Stripping off his filthy clothes, Evan pulled off his socks, bills fluttering to the floor. Putting everything in a pile with the bills stuffed in a sock, Evan stepped naked into the shower, turning on the water. Dirt and grime slipped away, washing down the drain. Finding a bottle of shampoo in the corner, he washed his long blond hair, unable to remember the last time he'd had his hair cut.

Evan jumped when he heard the outside door open and braced himself, placing his hands against the tile. So this was how it was? He'd played this game before, many times. Lots of guys who took him home liked to let him clean up before meeting him in the shower. "Father Valentin asked me to bring in some clothes for you," a quiet, unseen voice said, and Evan heard someone move around on the other side of the curtain. Peering out, he saw a man set a bundle on the counter before leaving the room again. Shaking his head, wet hair flopping on his shoulders, Evan finished his shower before stepping out. Towels rested on the counter along with the clothes and a small plastic bag of toiletries. His meager possessions remained where he'd left them. Drying himself, he pulled on the new clothes, trying not to look at himself as he combed his hair. Putting on his own shoes, Evan picked up his old clothes and left the bathroom, wondering where he should go. "Are you ready?" Evan jumped at the same voice that he'd heard in the bathroom. "Sorry," the young man said, "Father Val got called away, and he asked me to take you to meet our evaluator."

"What's that?" Evan inquired softly.

"Brother Benedict will test where you are academically so we can place you in the proper classes." The young man walked toward the door.

"Who are you?"

"Oh." The young man actually giggled. "I'm Brother Timothy. I'm the newest member of the order." He didn't seem that much older than Evan. "We shouldn't keep Brother Bart waiting." Evan followed Timothy through the halls and up two flights of stairs to a tiny room where he spent the next few hours working problems and reading out loud as well as taking all kinds of tests before Timothy returned. "Let's get you settled."

Evan followed Timothy out of the building and along a covered hallway to another building. Inside, Evan was led up more stairs and down yet another long, straight hallway. Heads turned inside rooms with open doors, and some of the other boys murmured quietly as he passed. Evan knew they were talking about him. Keeping his eyes down, he nearly ran into Brother Timothy when the young man stopped at one of the doors. "What's this?"

"This," Timothy started to say as he opened the door, "is your room. You'll share it with one other student."

Evan stepped forward and walked inside. The black-haired boy from the chapel looked up from his book, smiling at him.

Evan blinked a few times, his belly seizing hard, and for a second he thought he might be sick, but it settled to a dull ache. Evan didn't know what it meant, but felt fairly confident it had something to do with those huge eyes looking at him. Evan actually looked at Brother Timothy to see if he felt it, but his expression hadn't changed. "Hi," the boy said as he stood up, extending his hand. "I'm Clay Mueller, and you must be Evan."

Not knowing what else to do, Evan reached for the outstretched hand, and his bundle of old clothes slipped from his other hand, landing in a pile on the floor. "I'll take those to the laundry," Tim said, picking them up. Evan panicked as he saw his socks with all his money in it moving away. That small stack of bills was everything he had in the world, and if things didn't work out here…. Hurrying after the young brother, Evan grabbed for his ragged socks as he reached the door. His fingers feeling the bills, Evan clutched the socks as he saw Clay staring at him. Trying to get his heart to stop pounding, Evan gripped the bits of fabric like lifelines and watched as Brother Timothy disappeared from view.

"I take it those socks are special," Clay said, and Evan turned to him for a brief second before lowering his eyes to the floor, still holding the bits of fabric with everything he owned inside them. "Sorry," Clay said, and Evan sat on the edge of what he guessed was his bed, since it was the only one made and that half of the room appeared empty. The mattress sank beneath him, and Evan peered around the room, which consisted of two beds, dressers, and desks, along with a closet and window. "Father Val said you've had a hard time of things," Clay commented, and Evan lifted his eyes, finding Clay looking back. That seemed like the understatement of the century to Evan, but he wasn't in any mood to comment. He was still trying to figure out who, or what, had brought him here. "Not much of a talker? That's okay," Clay continued. "My mom says I talk enough for eight people, so we'll get along fine." Evan felt the bed dip as Clay sat next to him. "This is your bed," Clay went on. "You probably know that already, and that's your dresser. I put the uniforms and clothes brother Tim brought in the drawers. And that desk is yours, and you have half the closet, although I have to warn you, it's more like a quarter because my mom keeps sending more stuff, and I'm running out of room."

Evan looked away from his shoes, watching Clay as he talked on. He wasn't sure if Clay was really talking to him or just talking. "Okay," Evan said, not really caring, since his meager possessions would probably fit in one drawer of the white painted dresser.

"Hey, Clay." Another boy bounded into the room, and Evan saw him staring at both of them. "How long before you drive this one away? Clay hates having roommates and always finds a way to drive them away," the boy with wavy brown hair and a big nose went on to explain.

"Knock it off, Bryson," Clay said, jumping from the bed, grabbing the kid around the neck before running his knuckles over his head as they both began laughing.

Evan stood up. "I'll just go," he said softly. He should have known this was too good. He wasn't going to fit in, not here. The only place he fit was on the streets, like the whore he was. At least there he knew what to expect and could see things coming. Here, he never knew what to expect about anything. His socks still in hand, Evan walked out of the room and down the hall, toward the far door, hoping he could find Brother Timothy to get his clothes back. He had some money; he could use it to get back to where he belonged.

"Hey." He heard running behind him. "Evan, wait up." He kept walking and then felt someone tug on his arm. "Where are you going?" That was a good question. He could have answered "home," but he didn't have one. He'd spent months wandering, sleeping anywhere he could find. "Come on." He felt Clay tug him back toward the room. "Don't listen to Bryson. He's a complete moron." Back in the room, Clay shut the door like his new roommate was going to try to escape. "Do you want to talk about what happened to you?"

Evan shook his head. "Not really."

"That's okay. You don't have to tell me, you know." Clay flitted around the room, picking up some of the scattered clothes and pulling the covers up on his bed. "You know what I think?" Clay asked as he continued moving. "I think we're going to be good friends." A chime sounded outside the room, and Clay straightened his clothes. "Dinner's in five minutes," Clay announced. "You should put your things away, and we'll go."

Looking around, Evan realized the only thing he had to put away was his socks. Opening the top dresser drawer, Evan set the socks under the other clothes and shut the drawer. The sound of footsteps in the hall drew his attention, and Clay opened the door, waiting for him.

"Don't worry, everything will be fine." Clay stepped into the hallway, and Evan followed, joining the throng of other boys as they made their way down the stairs. At one point, he lost sight of Clay, and with everyone wearing the same thing, he couldn't pick him out. Evan followed the crowd and found himself in a large dining room. All the other boys lined up and appeared to be waiting. He felt a nudge on his arm and saw Clay standing next to him, giving him a smile. Peering around at the other boys dressed identically, he realized they all looked the same. Looking down at his own clothes, Evan realized he looked like everyone else—well, sort of.

All the boys bowed their heads, becoming quiet, and Evan saw Father Valentin standing near one side of the room. Evan followed suit, and he heard what sounded like a prayer. As soon as the prayer ended, doors opened and everyone talked at once, well, everyone except him. Following Clay, Evan picked up a tray and did whatever Clay did.

Carrying his full tray back out into the room, he sat next to Clay, and soon other boys joined their table. "Guys, this is my new roommate, Evan. That's Pete," Clay said, pointing, "Patrick, Wilbur, Dex, and the guy on the end is Frankie."

Evan felt a little overwhelmed. *Would these guys like him or hate him on sight?* Sometimes he half expected he had the word "whore" embossed into his forehead and that everyone knew what he'd been doing to survive. "Hi," he said tentatively.

"Father Val helped out Frankie too," Clay offered, and Evan looked at the other boy sitting at the far edge of the table.

"My folks couldn't afford the tuition, and Father Val arranged for a scholarship," Frankie offered with a pleased smile. "Father Val helps everyone he can. There are other guys here that he's helped too," Frankie said, pointing around the room before turning back to the table. "It takes some getting used to, but this is a good school, and most of us can go on to really good colleges," Frankie said with a smile on his face.

College was out of the question as far as Evan was concerned. He just needed to get through each day. The streets had taught him not to look forward to tomorrow, but to just try to live through each day as it came. "So this is for real?" Evan asked, directing the question to Frankie. "He's really that nice and doesn't want nothin'?"

All the boys around the table turned to where Father Valentin walked among the tables. Evan saw him stop at almost every table, talking to the boys, sometimes laughing, sharing a hug with some, especially what looked like the younger boys. Then he saw him walk closer, approaching their table. "Evening, boys," he said jovially.

"Hi, Father Val," seemed to be the most common response, and Evan saw the other boys smile at the priest, genuinely happy to see him. "You've all met Evan?" They nodded in response. "Excellent. I'd appreciate it if you'd show him around. Clay, we've placed him in many of your classes." He pulled out a printed page and handed it to Evan. "Clay will help you get to your classes tomorrow," Father Val told him. "Now, boys, I know I'm asking a lot here, but could you refrain from the usual initiation pranks? Evan needs to settle in, and I'd appreciate it if we could forego those, at least until he's had a chance to feel like one of us." All the boys nodded, and a few of them suppressed smiles. "Thank you, boys. I'll see some of you at bed check." Father Val gave them a smile, and Evan felt a hand rest on his shoulder, fingers squeezing lightly. Looking up, he saw the priest smile genuinely at him, and Evan's breath caught at the look on the man's face. He hadn't seen that since his dad had told him good night the day before…. Turning away, Evan looked down at his tray, unwilling to let the others see what he was feeling.

Laughter around the table pulled his attention back to the others, and he saw milk flowing down Frankie's face as one of the other boys patted his back. Evan felt himself smile, remembering what that was like. Taking a bite of food from his plate, Evan pushed away some of his feelings as he listened to the other boys, watching them have their fun, noticing that they included him. As they told their jokes, they waited for him to laugh too. One of the boys farted loudly before saying something about there being a duck under the table. Evan found himself smiling and then laughing, hard and strong, feeling the first bit of his worry begin to slip away just a little, and when his turn came, he told a joke he remembered his dad telling about a toothbrush salesman. The boys listened and then burst out laughing at the punch line.

Evan saw one of the brothers walk toward their table, a stern look on his face, and Evan turned back to his plate. As the brother approached the table, Evan saw Father Valentin steer him away. Evan wasn't sure the others saw, but he could have sworn Father Valentin winked at him as he steered the brother toward another table.

All the boys finished their dinner, bussing their trays before leaving the room. Evan once again did as Clay did before following him back to their room. Clay turned on the light before stripping off his uniform. Changing into sweats and a T-shirt, he flopped onto his bed with one of his books. "You want one?" Clay asked, lobbing a book at him. "This is our first class in the morning," Clay explained before telling him the assignment.

Evan sat at his empty desk and opened the book. Clay passed him a sheet of paper, and Evan began to work his way through the problems. Math had always been easy for him, and this seemed familiar, but every few minutes, he found himself peeking at Clay. Finishing the problems, Evan turned to Clay to ask a question and saw him yawn, arms stretching over his head, shirt riding high, a strip of lightly tanned belly showing above his sweatpants. Evan turned back around, feeling himself react. He knew what that meant. He'd taken care of many other men with that reaction, but none of them had ever affected him like that. Clay handed him another book and explained the reading assignment. Evan plodded his way through it for a while until he yawned. "It's almost time for bed check," Clay announced, and he left the room, returning a few minutes later. "Bathroom's two doors down on the left. You better hurry or you'll wait forever."

Evan grabbed the small bag of toiletries he'd been given and walked down the hall to the bathroom, hearing laughter drift out from the other rooms. In the bathroom, other boys hurried around, cleaning up and doing their business, most dressed for sleep. Evan did his best to ignore everyone, brushing his teeth before hurrying back to his room. Clay was already in bed, and Evan stripped off his clothes, folding them carefully.

Sliding between the sheets, he turned out the light. A soft knock sounded and then the door opened. Father Val walked in, saying good night to Clay before stepping to Evan's bed. He looked up into the priest's kind face and smiled, finally allowing himself to believe and hope this was all real. He saw the priest smile back before patting him lightly on the shoulder and leaving the room.

"Good night, Evan," he heard Clay say as he rolled over.

"Night," Evan replied softly with a smile.

Chapter 2

"EVAN." He turned around and saw Frankie walking down the hallway. "Dex's dad sent him one of those radio-controlled helicopters for his birthday, and we're gonna try it out on the lawn after class. You wanna join us?" Frankie asked in his usual excited voice. Like Evan, Frankie didn't have much, but he always mustered a lot of enthusiasm for everyone else. "We've prob'ly only got a few weeks before it starts snowing."

Evan adjusted the books on his arm. "Sure, sounds like fun," he answered with a smile, covering for the intense grinding in his stomach, but since the start of his first fall term at St. Bartholomew's, he'd gotten used to that. It was just part of his life now. At least in a few hours it would be behind him for another day or so.

"Then we'll see you out in the clearing near the old orchard," Frankie called with a wave as he hurried to his first class. Evan continued toward his own class, stopping outside the room, waiting for Clay because he didn't want to go in any sooner than he needed to. His first spring term at St. Bartholomew's had been better than he could ever have hoped. He had friends—good friends— something he'd never dreamed of having while he lived on the streets, and for spring break, when all the kids went home, Clay had invited him to come stay with his family for the week. Even the summer had been nice, if quiet. He'd gotten to spend a lot of time with Father Valentin and had come to trust him almost like a parent. Hell, as far as Evan was concerned, Father Valentin was as close to a parent as anyone he had. Everything had been wonderful, better than he thought he had a right to hope for. So when the fall semester started, he just wasn't prepared. Evan knew he didn't fit in, not really. For one thing, there was his attraction to his roommate that he couldn't seem to help. His being gay didn't throw him in the least; he'd known that before he'd arrived. He'd even talked about it with Father Valentin, who had been supportive and understanding while at the same time cautioning him that any actual behavior would not be tolerated.

No, it was the fact that he thought of Clay all the time, and he knew he was developing feelings for his roommate that would never be returned. Besides, Clay was his best friend and his lifeline, of sorts. He had friends, more than he could ever remember having before, but it was Clay who watched out for him, just like he looked out for Clay. They were like brothers, and that relationship was worth more to Evan than anything in the world. So at night, when everything was quiet, Evan often thought of Clay. As Father Valentin told him once, he had impure thoughts, and a lot of them.

"Are you gonna go inside or stand in the hall all day?" Clay asked from next to him before pushing the door open. Evan took a deep breath before walking into the room. Stepping over the threshold, Evan could almost feel his defenses rising, walls he'd hoped he wouldn't need again. Sitting down across the aisle from Clay, Evan waited for the beginning of the class.

"Good morning," Brother Renier said, as he strode into the room. Somehow, though he was dressed as plainly as the other brothers, Brother Renier's clothes always seemed to be cut just a little better than everyone else's. "I have your papers, so please take your seats, and when you're quiet, I'll hand them out." He glared at the class, and everyone became quiet.

"He can't fault you this time," Clay said softly, earning a shush from Brother Renier as he continued walking through the classroom, passing back the papers. They'd worked on their papers together. As Renier got closer, Evan felt his stomach begin to flutter and roll, knowing what was going to happen. Brother Renier took a paper off the bottom of the stack, handing it to him.

"See me after class," he said softly before moving on. Evan looked down at his paper, a red D- written in the upper corner. Peering over, Evan saw Clay's paper with its A- written on it. Folding his paper to hide it, Evan tried to keep Clay from seeing.

"No way, dude," Clay whispered and got shushed again as Brother Renier began the rest of the class.

"Let's review the highlights of *Romeo and Juliet*," Brother Renier began, and Evan did his best to pay attention, not at all looking forward to the end of class. "Mr. Herbst, would you please begin at page thirty-four? You read Romeo, and Mr. Mueller, since he seems so talkative, can read Juliet." Clay stood up, and for a while, Evan listened as Clay read the female part, the words reaching into his heart, wishing someone would say things like that to him. But that would never happen, not now.

The bell rang signaling the end of class, and Evan stayed in his chair as all the other boys left the room. Clay closed his book and prepared to leave the room as well, stopping near the door to look back at him. Evan wanted to get up and follow Clay, but couldn't. "Mr. Mueller," Brother Renier warned, a hint of menace in his voice. "You don't need to be late for your next class." Evan saw him look at Clay and then back at him, making a shiver run down his spine. Evan noticed Clay giving him a final look before leaving the classroom, and Brother Renier walked to the door, closing it soundly. "Your work is not up to the standards set by this school or by the other students in this class," Brother Renier began as he walked back to Evan, his eyes locking on Evan. "We've spoken about this numerous times since the term began, and I'm afraid you need another lesson in what's expected of you." Evan swallowed, saying nothing, knowing what would come next. "I have no idea why Father Valentin allowed someone like you into this school, but you certainly have your uses, don't you, Evan?" Brother Renier asked as he stepped closer, leaning over Evan's desk, his face so close, Evan could smell the scent from the cinnamon toothpaste he'd used that morning.

"I don't want to do this," Evan said softly trying to get up from his desk, but Brother Renier placed his hand on his shoulder, holding him in the chair. "I never did," he added, almost in a whisper.

"Sure you did," Brother Renier countered. "Before you came here, you were a little whore working the streets, and now you think you're respectable." Renier shook his head. "Not after what you've done all semester you aren't." Evan found himself pulled to his feet, half carried, half dragged toward the supply closet in the back of the room. "With your history, no one will believe you didn't offer yourself to me." Evan found himself thrust into the closet as Brother Renier closed the door, standing in front of it, legs spread, shoving Evan roughly to his knees.

Evan felt his consciousness shifting like it always did, shutting himself off from everything around him. It was the only way he'd been able to do this on the streets, and it was the only way he could do it now. Only this time, it was so very different. Evan knew Clay would never have anything to do with him now, not if he or anyone ever found out about this. Every time he'd been forced to do this, Evan felt a little more of the happiness and contentment he'd experienced last spring and summer slip away, and all he could hear in his head were Brother Renier's words that he was a whore. *And how could Clay ever love a whore?* Regardless of that, every time this happened, Evan felt as though he were somehow being unfaithful to Clay, to his feelings for him, to his love for him.

Evan heard the sound of a zipper lowering, a belt jingling as it hung open. Suddenly, he was transported back to an alley, the last time he'd done this in the city, the time he'd actually gotten away. He could feel the cold seeping up his legs, the wetness beginning at his knees and working upward. He could smell the nearby Dumpsters and feel the pavement scraping his knees. Doing his best to shut himself off from everything that was happening to him, Evan tried to think back to last spring when he and Clay had gotten permission to go into town with Brother Timothy. He'd only expected it to be a chance to be away from the school, but they'd stopped for ice cream and at one of the parks, where the three of them had played catch until their hands hurt. Evan brought up every happy memory he could think of to try to counter what was happening to him, to blot out the names he was being called. The names, the words, those always seemed to be the worst. Every time Brother Renier did this to him, the words he called him were always the hardest thing to wipe from his memory.

His throat hurt, eyes watered, and Evan continued playing every happy image he could think of, except one. He'd never let himself show any of the images of Clay. Those he didn't want tainted by what he was and by what he was doing. Evan gagged and began to cough as his images faded and he snapped back to the here and now. Without thinking, he spit and opened his eyes, seeing white gunk staining the front of Brother Renier's pants. "You little shit," Brother Renier growled and drew his hand back. Evan almost hoped he would hit him, but he didn't. Instead he reached for a roll of paper towel, blotting his own juices from his beloved pants. Evan watched as his teacher, a person he should have been able to trust, pulled up his zipper and fastened his belt, straightening his slacks before opening the door and stepping out of the confined space without looking back at him.

Placing his hands over his eyes, Evan felt the tears start to come. He forced himself to remain quiet, waiting until he heard the outer door close before allowing himself to actually shed his tears.

Searching for the paper towels, Evan wiped his eyes and slowly got to his feet. He walked out of the closet and went to his desk. The grade on his paper had been changed to an A-, and a hall pass sat next to it. Picking up both along with his bag, he wiped his eyes one more time before dropping the paper towels in the trash as he opened the door to the classroom, stepping out into the blessedly deserted hallway.

Stopping in the bathroom, Evan splashed water on his face before drying it. He hurried down the hall and opened the door to his math class, handing the instructor the pass before taking his usual seat next to Clay's. "Mr. Donaldson, do you have your homework?" Mr. Gerhardt asked. Evan dug in his bag, handing him the sheet before quietly getting out his class materials while the instructor continued his lesson. Evan tried to concentrate on what the instructor was saying, but he could feel Clay's eyes on him, and he forced himself not to look at him. Evan knew Clay would read everything that had happened on his face, and he couldn't bear the rejection of his friend if he knew what had been happening. Evan kept telling himself that it wasn't his fault, but deep down he knew it must be. Brother Renier hadn't told him anything that wasn't true, and no matter what he wanted to think, how many friends he had, or how hard he tried to fit in and act happy, he was still just a whore who had sold himself on the streets for food.

"What happened?" Clay asked, leaning across the aisle while Mr. Gerhardt's back was turned.

"He said he'd made a mistake," Evan answered, showing Clay the changed grade before doing his very best to focus on the class.

Evan could barely concentrate in the class he loved most of all. Tears threatened constantly as he thought about the past month or so. He knew what he had to do. He had to leave the school. The thought made his throat so tight he could barely breathe, but he couldn't see any other choice. On the streets at least he had some sort of control. He could decide who he went with, but here, he had no control at all. He was completely at Brother Renier's mercy, and he hated every minute of it. Peering to his right, he caught a glimpse of Clay looking back at him—his friend, the best friend he ever had. The thought of leaving and never seeing Clay again tore at his heart. Being Clay's roommate, seeing him every day along with the rest of his friends, was almost worth staying for.

"Mr. Donaldson." Evan heard his name and lifted his head, realizing every face in the class had turned to him. "Can you work the problem on the board?" Evan somehow stood up, feeling his legs shake beneath him as he took tentative steps toward the blackboard at the front of the class. Reaching it, his back to the class, Evan picked up a piece of chalk from the tray and took a deep breath. He could feel the entire class waiting for him, but he did his best to put it out of his mind. "Evan," he heard the instructor say softly, "is anything wrong?"

Evan shook his head and stared at what looked to him like white scribbles on the board. Taking a step back, he wiped his eyes and forced himself to concentrate through sheer will. Lifting his hand, he began to work the algebraic problem. Feeling his hand shake, he made the first lines on the board and felt his mind begin to clear, the gears switching as the numbers rearranged themselves and another part of his brain seemed to switch on. The lump in his throat faded as he continued working the complicated problem. Step by step, order emerged from the chaos of his mind, and he finished the problem with a slight flourish on the answer. Looking toward the teacher, Evan saw him smile, and he returned to his seat as Mr. Gerhardt continued with the rest of the class.

By the time Algebra was over, Evan felt as though he had himself under control, the impact of the encounter with Brother Renier already being stored away behind the walls of his mind. To Evan, it seemed like the only way he could deal. Shut it away and try his best to think of something else. That was what he'd done for the past few months, and that was what he knew he had to continue to do, but it kept getting harder. "Ev," he heard Clay whisper once Mr. Gerhandt had given them their assignments. There was still time left in the class, and they were to work on their assignments quietly. "You okay?"

Nodding his head, Evan pulled out his notebook and began writing out the first assigned problem. Numbers had always spoken to him, and thankfully today was no exception. Working the first one with ease, he continued to the next. Each one got progressively harder and more complex. As he worked them, Evan's mind continued to clear, focusing on unraveling the problem at hand, rather than on what had happened to him with…. Evan wouldn't even let his mind ponder or consider what had happened earlier. All that mattered was now, and he worked the problems with such fierce concentration that he almost didn't hear the bell at the end of class.

Lifting his head, Evan gathered his things and hurried out of the room. "Ev, wait up," Clay called from behind him, and he slowed. "Are you mad at me or something?"

Evan softened his expression, covering for the turmoil that still whirled inside. The last thing he wanted was for Clay to think he'd done something wrong. "No." Evan smiled at his friend. "I'm just thinking, that's all." The warning bell rang. "We better not be late for Religion," Evan said, and together they walked to their next class.

In the room, Evan sat in his usual seat, his breathing measured. To his surprise, instead of Brother Joda, their usual teacher, Father Val entered the room, closing the door. "Brother Joda is ill and won't be able to teach your class today, so I'll be taking his class," Father Val explained with a smile as he walked toward the desk. "I don't get to do this much anymore," he added with a smile. "I understand that you were reviewing the sacraments and were about to discuss Penance and Reconciliation. I know nearly all of you can recite what the catechism says, but I'd like to hear in your own words what this means to you." Father Val looked around the room, but Evan felt that no matter where he looked, his eyes seemed to zero in on him.

A boy in the front row raised his hand, and Father Val nodded to him. "It means confessing what you've done wrong."

Father Val nodded slightly. "Yes, it does, but it's more than that. In the church, we've formalized the process over the centuries, and with that formality, we've lost some of the true meaning." Father Val moved to stand behind the small lectern. "When you've done something wrong, you know it, don't you?" Evan felt himself nodding in agreement as did most of the boys in the room. "And how do you feel when you know you've done something wrong?" Father Val asked before answering his own question. "You feel bad about it." More nods. "But how do you fix it?"

"You go to confession," Frankie offered from his chair a few rows over.

"Yes," Father Val agreed. "But there's more to it than that. When you sin, you break your relationship with God, and we believe that relationship then needs to be repaired. Confession is the first part of the repair process," Father Val continued, and Evan found himself unusually interested in this particular topic. "Confession is accomplished between your priest, yourself, and God. Once you've confessed your sin, you need to atone for it, and that's the reconciliation portion of the sacrament, reestablishing your relationship with God. The confession portion is easy; the reconciliation portion takes reflection upon your behavior and making the appropriate changes in your life. That can often be hard, but meaningful change is never easy."

"What if you see the sin in others?" Frankie asked quietly from his seat.

"Enabling someone else's sin is just as bad as committing the sin yourself." Father Val seemed to stumble just a little. "You should discuss it with them to help them make the proper confession so they can be forgiven. That's part of why we're all here, to help each other, because in the faith, we are our brother's keeper." Father Val held up his hand to still the class from the undercurrent of chatter that erupted. "However, there are situations that you should not handle yourself. If another person is hurt or being hurt, the best you can do to help them is to consult with someone with more experience. That may be me, or another of the brothers, your parents, and sometimes the authorities."

"What about the stories about priests in the news? How does that fit into the sacrament? Are there times when it shouldn't apply?" one of the boys asked from the back. Evan couldn't see who it was, but found himself thinking very deeply about this very subject.

Father Val walked around to the front of the desk, leaning against the edge. "You're all bright young men with incredible futures ahead of you, and you see the news. We do not keep it from you. The church has been in the news a lot lately and not in a good way. The sacrament of Penance and Reconciliation has been used in cases where it shouldn't, not because the sacrament is wrong, but because the sinner confessing his sin wasn't penitent and didn't change his behavior. The sanctity of the confessional is sacred, but there are times when it may not be enough. Penance and Reconciliation is basically about taking responsibility for your sin, asking God to forgive you, and then atoning for it so you can reconcile yourself back to God." The bell sounded, and Evan thought Father Val looked relieved that the class was over. Evan, on the other hand, had so many questions he wasn't quite sure where to turn.

Remaining in his seat, Evan watched as the other boys left the room. He saw Clay get up, but noticed his friend waited with him. "Can I help you two?" Father Val asked softly.

Evan looked to Clay and back to Father Val. He had plenty of questions, but he didn't want to ask them now and definitely not in front of Clay. In the end, Evan shrugged and remained silent before heading for the door. Instead of turning to the right to follow the quickest route to the chapel, Evan turned left and hurried along the hall, making for the fresh outside air.

"Where are you going?" Clay asked, concerned. "We should be heading for mass."

Evan whirled around. "You go to mass. I just can't right now. I'll confess it later," he sniped, making his way toward the dorm. Evan wondered if Brother Renier ever discussed the things he made him do in that fucking closet during his confession. "How would that go?" he muttered under his breath to himself. "I make the little whore Evan Donaldson suck my cock so he can get the grades he deserves on his assignments. That'll be three Hail Mary's, two Rosaries, and tell me what it's like." Evan actually swished his hand around, smacking Clay on the chest as his anger and frustration built. He hadn't even remembered he was there. Hurrying inside the building, Evan made his way to their room, closing the door quietly behind them, tossing his books onto the bed before joining them with a bounce of the mattress.

He heard Clay moving around, setting his books on the desk. "You never skip class or mass," Clay said softly. "Are you sick?"

Evan rolled away, facing the far wall, unable to look at Clay, his anger flowing away, shifting to sadness mixed with pity and a healthy dose of self-loathing. "Yes, I'm sick. If you listen to Brother Renier, I'm one sick fuck," Evan answered, the words barely a whisper as he felt tears fill his eyes and slide down his cheeks, wetting the pillow.

"Do you want me to get the nurse?" Clay asked softly, and Evan felt him sit on the edge of the bed.

"No," Evan answered, his voice wavering. "I'm not that kind of sick."

"Is it Brother Renier?" Clay asked quietly, and Evan tensed, but said nothing. "There's something going on, I know there is. Every time he has you stay after his class, you get moody for the rest of the day." Evan felt Clay touch his shoulder, and he tried to make himself pull away, but he couldn't. Clay's hand felt so good. Evan sniffed and slowly rolled over, Clay's eyes searching into his. The urge to reach out and pull him close was so strong, it took the last of his will to stop himself. He desperately wanted to know what Clay's lips tasted like, what it would feel like to hold him and be held, to run his fingers through soft hair and to explore the body he'd seen, usually in the dark of night, just once. He'd be happy with once; he could live with once. Evan closed his eyes and let his brief fantasy take hold before opening them to reality once again. Clay had never given him the slightest inclination that he was interested in anything other than friendship. Besides, Clay deserved someone better than some cocksucking whore.

"What did he do to you?" Clay's question whisked away the last of his illusion like smoke in the wind. "I know he did something. Did he hurt you? 'Cause I'll kick his sick fuck ass if he did."

"Clay...," Evan said softly before his voice petered away.

"Did he hit you with that cane he keeps in the closet?" Evan shook his head, not able to get the words out. "What did he do? I know he did something, and today isn't the first time." Clay rubbed his arm softly. "There have been rumors about him," he said, and Evan blinked, almost unable to believe his ears.

"What about him?"

"I heard it from Gooding last week. He's one of the seniors, and he mentioned that he'd heard that you didn't want to be alone with Renier. He only said anything because he heard I had him this year. I asked him if he knew why, and he shook his head." Clay stopped and searched his expression. "I thought it was just one of those stories, but it isn't, is it?"

Evan stared up at Clay, eyes locking on his friend as he decided what to do. His first thought was to turn away again and say nothing. He knew he'd have to explain what had been happening, and the thought of telling Clay nearly made him sick, but he could barely hold in everything he was feeling right now. And almost before he knew what he'd done, Evan found himself nodding just slightly. "Yes," he squeaked out before burying his head in the pillow, trying to block out all the filthy names Brother Renier had used and the thought of what he'd done. But the genie was now out of the bottle, and Evan finally let loose everything he'd been carrying inside for weeks. His pillow absorbed the streams of tears while muffling the wrenching sobs that flowed out of him.

Hands stroked along his back, and at first Evan barely noticed, but soon the touch increased in intensity, and he realized that Clay was comforting him. He'd almost expected his friend to pull away. "What did he do?" Clay asked softly.

Evan rolled over and opened his mouth before jumping off the bed. Running out of the room and down the hall, he made it to the bathroom before losing everything he'd had for breakfast. Behind him, he heard the door open and close before Clay's hand rested on his shoulder and a paper towel dangled in front of him. Taking the towel, Evan wiped his mouth before standing on unsteady legs, moving to the sink to rinse away the acid taste before turning back to Clay. When he did, Evan felt his breath catch as he saw what looked like lines of tears running down his friend's face. "He kept giving me low grades, and when I asked him about them the first time, he showed me how I could raise them." Evan swallowed, not really wanting to say anything more. He wasn't really sure he could without being sick again, and just fell silent.

"Like today?"

Evan gasped for breath and nodded. "We worked together and should have gotten the same grade, but it wasn't until I...." Evan covered his face with his hands, feeling like he just wanted to sink through the floor.

"This is not your fault," Clay said softly, and Evan felt himself being pulled into a hug, arms encircling him, holding him. Evan would have given anything for the last year to have Clay hold him, but not like this. Resting his head on Clay's shoulder, he pressed his eyes closed and tried his best to not think about how much he'd wanted Clay to touch him or hold him, and he just let himself be comforted. "I mean it, Evan. This is not your fault. It's Brother Renier's fault, and he has to answer for it."

"What am I supposed to do about it?" Evan asked softly before straightening up, feeling Clay's arms slip away.

"I don't know, but let's get back to the room, and we can try to figure stuff out." Clay walked toward the door, and Evan followed, still wiping his eyes, as they walked back toward the room.

"Why aren't you boys at mass?" Evan turned around and saw Brother Timothy walking in their direction.

"Evan's sick. He was just throwing up in the bathroom. He thinks it's something he ate," Clay answered. The food at the school left something to be desired, and everyone knew it. The nuns who cooked were nice enough, but they definitely needed to take cooking lessons.

"I'm feeling better now," Evan said weakly and continued walking toward the room. He didn't hear what else Brother Timothy said, but Clay soon joined him, shutting the door.

"I know you're not going to like hearing this, but I think you need to tell Father Val what happened," Clay said, and Evan began shaking his head vehemently. He'd almost rather tell anyone else except him. "This is big, and he's the one who can handle it right. If we tell the rector, he'll just go to Father Val. Besides, as the head of the school, Brother Renier works for him. I'll go with you if you want," Clay offered, and in that moment, Evan looked at his friend and knew he loved him and would love him forever for that single gesture of support.

Evan knew this was something he had to do on his own. "I'll tell him," he said gently, drying his eyes one last time. "But I think we need to eat lunch. Well, you can eat lunch; I'll get something to drink."

"You sure?" Clay asked, walking toward the door.

"Yeah, I can't hide out here forever." Evan followed, and they made their way to the cafeteria.

Most eyes in the room turned as they walked in, not the least of which was Father Val, who made his way over to them almost immediately.

Evan looked to Clay, who nodded to him lightly as they both watched the priest cross the room. "Neither of you were at mass." He didn't ask a question, but Evan found himself answering anyway.

"I wasn't feeling well," Evan said softly, showing Father Val that he only had a small glass of apple juice. He felt Clay's elbow nudge him slightly, prodding him forward. "I need to talk to you."

"You know my door is always open. Come to my office during your free period, and we'll talk." Father Val looked at both of them in that funny way priests have, letting you know he wasn't exactly pleased with you, but seemingly letting you off the hook while telling you he's watching, all at the same time.

Evan nodded slowly and finished the juice, his stomach settling slightly. He was still keyed up, and his nerves were firing to the point he felt himself nearly start to shake, but he also felt a glimmer of hope. If Father Val believed him and took action, maybe this could stop, and maybe he could be happy again. As Evan mulled over everything, keeping his head down, eyes on the tabletop, Clay finished his lunch. A hand touched his shoulder, making him jump. "Sorry." It was Frankie, standing right behind him, smiling his usual bright smile. "We'll look for you after class to fly the helicopter?"

Some of Frankie's happiness rubbed off, for a few seconds, and he smiled at the super-intelligent younger boy. He liked Frankie; it was impossible not to. He was a year behind them, but took most of their classes because he was just that smart, and he approached everyone and everything with such outright enthusiasm. "We'll be there." Evan mustered some enthusiasm of his own, even if it only lasted until Frankie walked toward the door.

"Come on, just one more class and maybe this can be over," Clay said, picking up his tray. Evan knew that whatever he told Father Val, it wouldn't be the end, but just the beginning—of what, he had no idea. Picking up his glass, he followed Clay, placing the dirty dish in the tub before walking with him out of the cafeteria and toward their room to retrieve their books.

Their next class passed by incredibly fast, and with Clay's prodding, Evan found himself outside Father Val's office door, looking around before nervously knocking. He heard Father Val call for him to enter, and he pushed the door open.

"Evan, how can I help you?" Father Val asked as he stood up from behind his desk. Evan took a step forward before closing the door, taking a deep breath, unsure where to start, or how to tell him what he needed to. "Something is obviously troubling you. Today's the first time you've ever skipped mass, and I've never known you to not be hungry, either." Father Val winked. "So why don't you sit down and talk to me."

Evan lowered himself into one of the chairs across from Father Val's desk. "I'm not sure how to tell you this," Evan started to say, "but it's about Brother Renier."

"I know you've had some problems in his class this year. But if you apply yourself, you can do better."

Evan shook his head. "It's not that. Well, yes, I guess maybe it is, sort of." Evan heard himself rambling, but his nerves were quickly getting the best of him.

Father Val held up his hand. "Relax and start at the beginning," he said patiently.

Evan took a deep breath and released it very slowly. "A week or so after the start of classes, I stayed after class to ask him for some help because my grades weren't as good as I wanted." He'd always worked very hard and studied hard, as though he needed to prove to himself that Father Val's kindness in helping him wasn't in vain. "And he offered to help me. I found out fast that his help came with a price." Evan felt his words start to flow faster. "Brother Renier found out somehow about what I'd done in the city, and he decided that was what he wanted for his help."

Evan stopped and peered up at Father Val, whose eyes had widened. "Whenever he'd give me a bad grade, if I stayed after class, he'd take me into the supply closet and…." Evan felt his throat and mouth go dry—he couldn't describe what Brother Renier had made him do, not to Father Val. Not to the person he thought of almost like a father. Suddenly he was back in that tiny space, on his knees, and he felt himself begin to shudder and shake. "Afterwards he'd give me a different grade on my papers." Evan stopped for a second, silent at the look of horror on Father Val's face. "The grade I should have had all along. He was marking me down so he could force me to"—Evan swallowed—"service him."

Father Val said nothing, and Evan couldn't read a thing in his expression other than surprise and horror.

"I didn't want to do it, Father Val. I really didn't. You've been so good to me, and you told me the rules, and I obeyed them and always did what you asked me to do." Evan stared at his shoes, unable to look at Father Val's expression any longer, and waited for him to say something.

"You traded sexual favors for grades?" Father Valentin asked softly.

"No, it wasn't like that. He forced me. I didn't want to, honest," Evan cried, jumping out of the chair, hurrying to Father Val, who actually stepped back. "I didn't. He was grading me down to…." Evan's words died in his throat as he looked up at the priest, seeing the shock and pity on his face. "You don't believe me?" Evan asked, barely out loud. "He used me, and you don't believe me."

Father Val looked like a statue, unmoving, as Evan watched the priest stare at him. "I…," Father Valentin started to say, and then his mouth clamped shut, eyes still wide as though he couldn't quite believe what he was hearing, or just didn't want to believe it.

Evan glanced around the office, trying to think of a way to convince Father Valentin that he was telling the truth. Hurrying to the desk, he snatched a Bible off the corner, clutching it. "I'm telling you the truth," he pleaded, his hands shaking as he held the sacred book. "I've never lied to you," he added, imploring Father Valentin to believe him. Evan waited, but Father Val seemed stunned into inaction, and Evan knew what that meant. He saw the blank look and backed away, almost unable to believe that the priest, the man he'd come to think of as a father, didn't believe him. He truly was trapped, and he saw no way out.

Anger welled inside him, deep-seated anger from the abuse, and shock at what he viewed as Father Valentin's betrayal of his love. Lifting the book, he flung it to the floor, the cover smacking the wood, sounding like a gun shot. "God is dead!" Evan shouted. "It's all a bunch of shit. He died the same day my parents died, and you buried him today!" he shouted as he grabbed his books from the table beside one of the chairs. "I'll never set foot in that church of yours again!" Hurrying from the office before Father Valentin could respond, he nearly knocked Brother Timothy to the floor as he slammed the door behind him, taking off as fast as his feet could carry him.

"Evan!" Hearing Clay's voice behind him, he slowed, his legs eventually coming to a stop. "What happened?" Clay asked as he approached. Evan turned, and Clay gasped. "He didn't believe you?" Evan shook his head, wanting a little more of the comfort Clay had offered him earlier, but he didn't know how to ask for it. "What are you going to do?"

Evan shrugged. "Leave, I guess." He felt as lifeless as a deflated balloon. He'd thought about doing just that so many times, but he couldn't figure out where to go. He didn't want to go back to the streets. He'd gotten a glimpse of what was possible. "I just don't know," he added, walking through the hall to his next class without really thinking about it.

"I'll meet you in our room after our last class," Clay told him, and Evan nodded slowly before walking into the classroom. His next classes passed in a blur. Evan couldn't concentrate on anything. He'd actually been called on and had merely stared blankly back at the instructor and shaken his head. The teacher must have taken pity on him, because he thankfully didn't dwell on it and moved on to another question. Blessedly, after his last class, Evan walked back toward the dorm and into the room, surprised to see not only Clay, but Frankie as well.

"Sorry, Frankie," Evan said softly, "I don't feel much like flying helicopters. You go and have a good time."

"He's not here for that," Clay corrected, his voice firm. "I saw the guys after class and asked them if they knew of anyone who'd had any trouble with Brother Renier. Most of the guys shook their heads, except Frankie."

Evan felt himself go white as he sat down hard on the edge of his bed. Frankie—sweet, smiling, happy Frankie? Evan found himself seething at the thought. "What happened?" Evan asked as his mind, which had finally returned to normal after the encounter with Father Valentin, began to race again.

Frankie didn't say anything, and Evan saw Clay nod his head. "It's okay, Frankie, neither of us will tell anyone unless you say."

"A few weeks ago, I stayed after class to ask a question, and he stood so close, like he always does, and I think he touched me. I'm not sure. And then he told me that if I needed special help, we could arrange to meet outside of class." Frankie looked like he was about to shake. "It felt creepy, and I left right away and never asked him for anything since." Frankie looked as though he might cry, and Evan knew exactly how he felt. "I didn't do anything wrong, did I? I mean, I didn't lead him on or anything."

Evan stood up. "No. You did nothing at all. It's Brother Renier who has the problem." Evan was finally coming to realize that. His past was irrelevant—it was Brother Renier who was abusing his position, and he was one sick fuck if he'd go after Frankie. "Like Clay said, we won't tell; we promise," Evan said and tried to smile. "Go have fun flying helicopters with Dex."

The door had barely closed behind Frankie when Clay began firing questions. "What are we going to do? Are you really going to leave? You can't. We have to do something!"

"Clay, I don't know what I'm going to do, but I have to tell Father Valentin that he's tried things with other boys too. I won't mention any names, but he has to know. Maybe he'll believe me now." Clay didn't seem convinced, and Evan wasn't, either, but he knew he had to at least try. All he could think was how many other kids had gone through this too?

Evan heaved himself off the bed and walked toward the door. "I'll see you at dinner." Pulling open the door, he left their room, the sound of the other boys talking and studying drifting into the hall. Everything sounded normal, and for them it was, and that was how it needed to stay, but it couldn't as long as Brother Renier was around. Briskly, he walked to the stairs and out into the twilight toward the academic building where Father Valentin had his office.

The hallways were mostly dark, but there was enough light for him to see where he was going as he made his way to the far end of the building. Steadying his nerves, Evan pushed open the restroom door, turning on the light before walking to the sink, splashing water on his face. The door closing again made him turn around. Brother Renier stood just inside. "I told you no one would believe you," he said, his voice dripping honey. "Not that it matters, because you know I'm only giving you what you want, what you need." He stepped closer, and at first Evan reacted the way he always had. He knew what was coming, and the walls around his mind began to rise, like they had all the other times. "You like it. Hell, you *want* it, and so do I." Brother Renier stood right near him, close enough that he could smell his breath.

Evan said nothing, finding himself riveted in place. "Besides, if it's just you and me then I won't need your little friends. Father Valentin didn't believe you, and they won't believe you either, you know that." His walls continued to build, and for a second, Evan could feel himself back on the streets, just like he always had before, his body and mind going on autopilot. An image of Frankie flashed into his mind, and that alone brought him back, the walls crashing away, the images fading, his defenses replaced by his own pent-up anger and frustration. This man standing in front of him, this bastard had taken everything, even his relationship with Father Valentin. "Don't worry, I'll be good to you," Brother Renier continued, the sweetness in his voice belied by the nearly feral look in his eyes. "You really do want it, don't you?"

Evan felt hands on his shoulders, pushing him down, and he let himself be moved, his knees meeting the tile. This time there was no wetness, no sound or smell from the streets. This time he was present, and Evan ground his teeth, nearly biting his lip to keep himself from growling. Brother Renier was bigger and stronger than he was, and he couldn't fight him directly, but he'd be damned if he was going to take it like he had before. This wasn't a secret any longer—Clay knew, and so did Father Valentin, whether he believed it or not. He knew or had at least been told, and Evan knew he could tell others if he had to. Clay hadn't rejected him, and that one thing alone helped make him strong.

Evan watched as the pants in front of him parted, the honeyed words continuing. He'd done this many times before, and he could do it again. Thoughts of his feelings for Clay swept through him, and he shuddered. He'd always been able to block them out before, push them behind the walls, but not this time. He'd always felt like he was betraying Clay, but now it was downright agony.

Lifting his hands off the tile, he let one glide over the shaft in front of him, looking up into the older man's face, stroking lightly, seeing his eyes glaze over and watching his head tilt back. "You know what to do," he crooned softly, and Evan nodded slightly. *That he did.*

Bringing up the fingers of his other hand, Evan grabbed hard, twisting, pulling, and yanking the tender flesh. Closing his eyes, he held on as he felt the other man drop to the floor, pushing him away. Letting go, Evan scrambled to his feet, looking at Brother Renier writhing on the tile floor. Evan lifted his foot, kicking his abuser in the back a couple times for spite.

"I'll get you, you little whore!" Brother Renier spat out.

"How? You'll have to explain my hands on your balls," Evan said, kicking the man hard one more time for good measure. "Father Valentin may not believe me, but the other kids will. Maybe we'll make up a nickname for you, Brother Blowjob." Evan made for the door, half surprised someone hadn't heard. Walking back, he couldn't resist one more kick, this time connecting with the hands covering the injured parts. The man's cries of pain mimicked the internal screams Evan had uttered in his head every time he'd been forced. He knew he shouldn't, but hearing the other man's pain made him feel better, allowing him to let go of some of his own guilt. He'd stood up for himself.

As Evan pushed his way out of the door, Brother Renier's moans filtered into the hallway before being cut off when the door closed. "Are you okay?" Clay asked as he rushed up to him. "I looked for you when you didn't come back."

Evan glanced toward the bathroom. "Let's get out of here." Evan walked through the building toward the entrance nearest their dorm, feeling free for the first time since classes started almost two months ago. Stepping outside, the door clanging closed behind them, Evan looked toward the stars, took a deep breath, and released a sigh.

"What happened?" Clay asked as they made their way toward the other building.

"I stopped in the bathroom to steady my nerves before talking to Father Val, and Brother Renier cornered me." Evan stopped, checking to make sure no one else was around. "I guess he thought I'd roll over like I had so many other times before, but this time I got angry. The thought of Frankie, or any of my friends, going anywhere near that monster…." Evan swallowed and stopped as he heard footsteps crunching on the leaves, waiting for them to pass by.

"What did you do?" Clay asked, and Evan could see his wide eyes in the reflected light.

"Let's just say he's going to be walking really funny for quite a while." Evan began to chuckle, which built into a full-on laugh as the last of the tension drained out of him. "I don't think Brother Blowjob will be bothering anyone very soon," Evan added before hurrying out of the cold night and inside to grab his coat. "We should get to dinner before there's no food left."

"Brother Blowjob," Clay repeated, chuckling as he elbowed him playfully in the side before opening the door to their dorm.

After dinner and studying, time for lights out arrived quickly, and after cleaning up, Evan climbed beneath his clean sheets. For whatever reason, he felt clean as well. "Are you going to tell Father Val what happened?" Clay asked after bed check.

"Maybe someday, but not now," Evan answered into the darkness of the room. "Thank you," he added after settling onto his pillow.

"What for?"

"Believing me." And for so very much more that Evan could not begin to put into words.

"Evan, are you gay?" Clay's voice sounded soft, like he wasn't sure he should ask the question.

"Yes," Evan answered matter-of-factly, and he waited for Clay's reaction. In his dreams of this moment, he'd always hoped Clay would tell him he was gay, too, and then slip into bed with him, where they'd make mad passionate love. God, he was such a dork, even in his fantasies. "Is that okay?"

"Of course," Evan heard from the other bed. "You're my best friend, and you always will be." Evan released the breath he'd been holding, relieved beyond belief before waiting to see if Clay would say anything more. He almost asked the same question back, but chickened out. Besides, if Clay were gay, he deserved someone better than someone with Evan's past, anyway. "Good night, Evan, you really rocked."

"Thanks, Clay, good night," Evan answered before the room became silent.

Chapter 3

THE overhead buzzing of the tiny helicopter engine had him looking toward the sky, looking for where the annoying toy was. "Hey, watch what you're doing. You nearly gave me a haircut with that thing," Evan called with a smile on his face as his friends had a ball. Sitting in the shade of a nearby tree, he watched as they ran and chased that infernal buzzing thing. He'd tried operating it once, and they'd nearly lost it in the orchard.

Frankie raced over, smiling as usual. "Can you believe it? Dex said I could keep the helicopter." The younger boy still had one more year, and Evan knew Frankie wasn't keen to see them all graduate. They'd all been inseparable friends for almost three years now. "I'm going to miss all of you next year," he confessed as Evan watched him dig a hole in the scrubby grass with his foot.

"We'll see each other again, you know that," Evan replied with a smile, knowing exactly how Frankie felt. Leaping forward, Evan grabbed for his friend, pulling him onto the grass, the two of them suddenly wresting on the lawn, laughing and carrying on.

After the abuse at the hand of Brother Renier, for the longest time, Evan had found it hard to just be himself. For months he'd examined every look, every touch he'd received from one of the instructors or the brothers. It took time and a lot of support from his friends, who eventually wormed the story out of him, but he got back to what passed for normal and found he could have fun again and that he didn't have to worry about every little thing.

Brother Renier had walked funny for weeks, and at the end of the semester announced that he was leaving the school. No one had shed a tear, especially Evan. In a closed, close-knit community, a secret doesn't stay secret for long, and soon a few rumors circulated as to why Brother Renier was leaving. There weren't details attached, but those weren't necessary. It was enough that Brother Blowjob, as he and Clay referred to him, was gone for good. The one thing the whole incident had done for Evan was to make him extremely self-reliant and strong. He knew he could handle most anything now.

Frankie stopped fighting back, and Evan rested on the ground, both of them panting, with huge grins on their faces. "You're getting stronger," Evan said to Frankie. "Next year you'll rule the roost."

"I'd rather go to college with you than stay here all alone," Frankie replied softly, picking at a blade of grass as Dex whizzed the helicopter overhead, sending Evan diving for cover and the others into fits of laughter. "Have you decided what you're doing after graduation?" Frankie asked, once the helicopter passed overhead. "I heard you got accepted to lots of colleges."

"Yeah, well, it doesn't matter. I can't afford any of them, so I guess I'll have to get a job. Father Val said I could stay here during the summer and help with the summer action retreats for new students, but I think it's time to move on. I've been here for almost three years, and I doubt anything will change by the end of summer. One of the brothers asked if I was interested in joining the order, but no. I'm gay, and the last thing they need is another person using the order to hide."

"You're gay?" Frankie said with mock indignation and a rude hand gesture, reducing them both to laughter once again. Evan had told all his friends he was gay shortly after the whole incident with

Brother Renier. But he hadn't made it generally known, and his friends had honored his privacy. He had told Father Valentin at one point, because although he already knew anyway, it just seemed like the right thing to do. He and Father Valentin had had less and less contact over time, and Evan knew that was because of him. He hadn't been able to forgive the priest for not believing him. He knew he should, and he'd thought about it often. A few months ago, he'd realized the anger, guilt, and frustration with his guardian had mostly faded away. Maybe it was time after all.

Of course Clay already knew he was gay, and it hadn't made a difference in their relationship. They were as strong of friends as ever, much to his relief. Evan knew he was still in love with his friend, but kept that to himself, his feelings locked away deep and only allowed to come out when he was alone or asleep. His dreams often starred his handsome roommate, but that's all they were… dreams. "You're the first gay person I've ever known," Frankie said, bringing Evan out of his own thoughts.

"No, I'm not. I'm the first you can talk about it with," Evan corrected lightly. "You've probably known lots of gay people, but didn't know they were gay, and that's good. You know you should treat everyone the same."

"I know," Frankie added, before asking, "but how do you know you're gay?"

"I don't know. How do you know you're straight?" Evan nudged his friend, wondering where this was coming from. "I guess it comes down to who you like. I like boys instead of girls. It's just part of who I am." Evan lifted his gaze and saw Clay taking over the controls of the helicopter. "Why?"

"I'm just curious, I guess."

Evan leaned closer, winking. "Is there something you want to tell me?" At first Frankie looked shocked and then he recovered, swatting Evan on the shoulder before laughing.

"Nah, I like girls," Frankie answered as he got up.

"Okay, just checking," Evan called as Frankie raced to where the helicopter was being piloted. Some things were good to know. That he had good friends like Frankie was definitely one of them. The helicopter buzzed close, and Evan took a halfhearted swat at it, looking at the gleeful expression on Clay's face. Clay—he was the person he'd miss most of all. Regardless of his feelings for him, they'd shared a room, their living space, for nearly three years. Going their separate ways as they would tomorrow felt like he was letting a part of himself go. He'd racked his brain trying to figure out how to go with him. Clay was going to college, and Evan had even applied to the same school. He'd been accepted, but even if he had the money, they didn't offer the programs Evan really wanted. Clay was going to be a lawyer; there was no doubt about that. His father and grandfather had been successful lawyers, and Clay was determined to follow in their footsteps. Evan's incident with Brother Renier only seemed to firm those ambitions for Clay.

"Hey, why are you sitting here all alone?" Clay asked as he appeared next to him, flopping onto the grass.

"Just thinking, I guess."

"I know you're worried, but things will work out. Father Val won't throw you out, you know that," Clay remarked, "regardless of what happened."

"I know. It's hard knowing you don't have much of a future." Evan looked around at the other guys. "Guess I'm feeling sorry for myself. Don't worry. It'll pass in a few years." He felt himself being tugged closer, and then knuckles ran lightly over his head.

"You're such a goof," Clay teased, releasing him. "You have a future, and you just have to find it."

"I just wish I'd hear about those scholarships. I got so many letters saying I was in the final groups, but haven't heard anything more. I actually thought about going into the Air Force, then they could pay for college. But knowing me and my big mouth, I'd probably tell, and then I'd get kicked out." Evan forced a smile. All the other students would go home to their families for a last summer before going off to college.

"You'll be fine," Clay encouraged him. "You're the strongest person I know, and you'll make something happen if you have to."

"Thanks, I needed that," Evan said. *That was enough of the woe-is-me shit.* He'd survived on the streets, and he'd taken care of Brother Renier—he could do anything he set his mind to. Tomorrow, he'd figure everything out. But today was graduation and their last day together before everyone left and everything changed. Getting up, Evan pulled Clay to his feet and joined the others.

"Evan," Dex called, taking back the helicopter controls, "glad you decided to join us." Dex twisted and turned along with the hovering craft, doing his best to keep it out of the trees. "I'd ask you if you'd like to take a turn, but we don't have all day to look for it."

"Smartass," Evan retorted, but he knew Dex was right. They'd probably never find it again if he took a turn.

All of them had become so very close. The previous summer, Evan had spent time with both Clay's and Dex's families. Clay's parents and sisters had been warm and accepting, making him feel very welcome in their comfortable home near Green Bay, just an hour away from the school. Dex's family lived outside Detroit, and Dex had invited him to come stay for a week. He'd even sent him a plane ticket. Evan knew Dex's family had money, but he'd had no idea how much until Dex picked him up at the airport and they rode back to the biggest house Evan had ever seen. The stone mansion was massive. Dex had explained that it had been built by his grandfather, who'd started the family business supplying parts to the infant auto industry, and they'd grown and expanded well beyond their roots.

"Don't let it get to you—we're just normal people," Dex had explained when he saw that Evan's jaw had dropped to the floor of the car as they pulled into the long driveway, passing a huge fountain and manicured, formal grounds in front of the elegant house. "There's nothing to be nervous about. My mother is going to love you," Dex added. "My parents are pretty cool, all in all."

It had been a good visit. Dex's dad had turned out to be a jovial man who worked a lot, but when he was home, seemed to spend time with the entire family. The Saturday they were there, he took everyone on an all-day sail on Lake Huron. Evan would never forget the way the sailboat skimmed across the water like it was part of the air. He and Dex had even climbed onto the front and done the "I'm the king of the world" thing from *Titanic*. It was cheesy and great fun.

"Are you staying here this summer?" Dex asked, pulling him back to the present. He'd found himself doing that a lot lately, remembering snippets of fun he'd had with his friends, like he was afraid he'd forget them.

"Don't know what I'm doing," Evan answered. "I'd love to do something with computers. Helping Mr. Gerhardt with the network designs for the school was really cool." Last summer, the school had decided it was time they brought their classrooms up to date and that it was time to computerize. Evan had worked with Mr. Gerhardt to help design and install the computer network connections with the electrical contracting company. More and more, Evan found that numbers and computers spoke to him at an almost instinctive level. Evan had loved that he'd been able to contribute to the school that had given him so much.

Dex gave him a sly grin as he landed the helicopter on the grass before checking his watch. "Lunch should be ready in a few minutes," Dex said, walking over to the aircraft, picking it up, and handing it along with the controls to Frankie, who beamed at Dex like he'd hung the moon.

"Thank you, Dex."

"You're welcome, Frankster," Dex teased and got a brief scowl from their friend before his usual smile returned full force. Evan watched Frankie carry his gift across the lawn, and with Evan waiting for Clay, they all made their way inside.

Yes, Evan had been happy here at St. Bart's. For most of his time here, he'd had a chance to thrive, but now that was all going to change. The outside world was calling, and it wouldn't be ignored.

In their room, he and Clay looked around. Boxes already packed were stacked in one of the corners. Most of them were Clay's; Evan had very little to pack. He'd accumulated a few things, but there wasn't a lot he was taking with him. The pictures they'd tacked to the walls were gone, as were their books. The desks looked blank and empty, like they were already waiting for next year's students. Evan found himself falling into another funk and did his best to push it away. Looking at his bed, he squinted when he saw an envelope resting near his pillow. Picking it up, Evan opened the manila folder and saw a letter inside. Looking back at Clay, Evan grinned and said, "When did this come?"

"This morning. Father Val asked me to give it to you," Clay said, smiling right back. "I didn't look at it, though," Clay added, and Evan felt him move closer. Whenever they were together in the room, his body seemed to know instinctively where Clay was, even in the dark without any sound.

"It's a scholarship letter from the order. They've awarded me two thousand dollars a year for the next four years to be applied toward tuition." Evan looked at Clay, confusion and elation fighting for dominance. "I never applied for this. I didn't even know this existed." Turning the letter over, Evan looked for something more, but found nothing other than some papers he needed to fill out and return. "Who...?" Evan started to say, as he wondered out loud.

"Who do you think?" Clay answered, and Evan felt the papers slip from his hands, the sheets falling to the floor. Evan scrambled to pick them up, trying ineffectually to cover his surprise. "Evan, Father Val cares for you a great deal. Everyone can see that. I know you think he didn't believe you, but he brought you here and has taken care of you for years," Clay told him, as Evan found himself staring at the pages. "Maybe you should make peace with him before you leave."

Evan knew Clay was right, but he didn't know what to say to the man he'd thought of as a father figure. "I don't know if I can. The things I yelled at him. They were terrible."

Clay didn't say anything. Instead he just gave him that look, and for a second Evan could see him in a courtroom giving a hostile witness that look, knowing they'd fold just like Evan could feel himself doing.

"Okay," Evan said, caving. "I'll talk to him, but after lunch. My stomach's about ready to start eating itself," Evan said before adding, "even for nun cooking." Both of them laughed. The food at the school was a running joke. The nuns who prepared the food were kind and very well-meaning, but some of the things they fixed were nearly inedible. Milk and vegetables were often brought in or donated from local farms and gardens, so that was always delicious. But sometimes….

"I will not miss nun peanut butter," Clay said as they walked the distance to the dining hall. In an effort to stretch the peanut butter, the nuns added oil to it and whipped it. The stuff was ghastly.

"How about nun surprise?" Evan asked with a chuckle as Clay shivered in the warm spring air. "You never knew what you were going to get in a casserole. Sometimes it wasn't too bad…."

"And sometimes you ate the plate instead," they finished together as Evan pulled open the door. Inside, lunch smelled really good, and Evan felt his stomach rumble. Getting in line, Evan picked up a tray, getting his lunch before walking to their table. His group of friends had eaten every meal at the same table since he'd come to the school. The overlapping voices sounded the same as they always did, but to Evan it seemed different, more musical, as he listened to it for the last time. The lunch conversation centered around their plans for the summer. Evan told them about the scholarship he'd received, and he saw Clay and Dex looking at each other knowingly, but neither said anything. Something was definitely up, but he knew he'd get nothing out of either of them until they were ready.

Frankie was the first to get up since he and the other juniors were on duty for graduation. Freshmen and sophomores were already gone since classes had ended last week. Soon the room cleared out, and Evan saw only the seniors lingering. "Parents will start arriving soon," Clay said softly. "If you want to talk to Father Val, you should do it now." Evan swallowed and took his tray. Emptying it, he placed the dishes in the tubs before waving goodbye.

Minutes later, he found himself outside the door to Father Val's office, and he knocked softly. "Come," he heard spoken from inside, and he pushed the door open. He hadn't been in here since…. Evan stopped himself from thinking about it or otherwise he'd never say what he felt he needed to.

"Evan," Father Val said as he smiled, putting down his pen before getting up from behind his desk. "I'm glad you stopped by."

"I thought there were some things we needed to talk about before I left," Evan said as he shifted slightly from foot to foot. The office looked the same, as did the Bible, back in its usual place on the corner of the desk rather than on the floor where Evan had hurled it the last time he was here.

"Yes, I think we do," Father Val commented softly before motioning toward the chairs. Evan sat and watched as Father Val did the same. "I know you don't think I believed you when you told me about Brother Renier, and truthfully, I can't tell you what I believed at the time." Evan opened his mouth, but Father Val held up his hand, and he closed it again. "All I can say is that I think I didn't want to believe someone like that could be teaching at the school." Father Val sighed. "I also know I let your past cloud my judgment, and for that I ask your forgiveness. There was no excuse for Brother Renier's behavior, ever, and for the record," he said as he actually looked toward the ceiling, "I know in my heart you did nothing wrong. My first obligation is to the boys under my care."

"It hurt, a lot," Evan said softly, some of the pain and humiliation of the abuse coming back to him. "What made you realize what was going on?"

Father Val shifted uncomfortably in the chair. "What's revealed in confession is sacred, but it doesn't have to be without consequence. But I will say you weren't alone in what you dealt with." Father Val swallowed hard. "I just wish I could have been there to help you through it."

"I had good friends who stood by me. They got me through." There wasn't a day he wasn't grateful for Frankie, Dex, Clay, and Wilbur. They'd rallied around him.

"Changing the subject, I wanted to thank you for the scholarship."

Father Val shook his head lightly. "You earned it. I put in the application, but the governing committee awarded it to you. I had no other influence whatsoever." Father Val seemed very pleased. "You were… are," he corrected, "an amazing student with a bright future ahead of you. Never doubt that. You always worked hard and deserved everything you received, and a lot more." Father Val sat back in his chair, becoming more comfortable now that the topic had shifted. "Have you decided where you're going to school?"

"Not really. Even with the scholarship, I don't see how I can afford it."

"There are loans and government grants you qualify for. I know you applied. The thing is, you need to decide where you're going, and then they'll work with you, believe me. Gifted minds like yours do not come along all the time. I'll be here when you need me. Just because you're leaving doesn't mean I won't be here for you."

Evan felt himself swallow around the huge lump in his throat. He'd wasted so much time being angry and feeling betrayed that he'd missed the time he could have had with this man who was more special to him than he'd realized. "Can I ask something?" Evan inquired, and Father Val nodded slowly. "Why me? There are so many other people who need help. Why did you choose me that winter day?"

Father Val smiled a small, innocent smile as he leaned forward. "I didn't." Father Val became quiet, letting his message sink in. "I wasn't supposed to be in that section of town. I'd never gone there before and I haven't since. It isn't near where we got the supplies for the school, and to this day I have no idea how I got there. I just found myself there and saw you." Father Val held up his hands the same way he did at the end of mass when he gave the final "Thanks be to God." "You should get ready," he said, lowering in hands. "Graduation will start in a few hours."

Evan stood up, and so did Father Val, who held out his hand. Ignoring it, Evan hugged the man who'd gotten him off the street and given him a chance at a life. "There's just one more thing I need to do," Evan said, and Father Val nodded. Slowly, Evan sank to his knees. "Forgive me, Father, for I have sinned…." Evan told him everything about the abuse, how long it had gone on, his own fears, and even what he did to Brother Renier, among other things he should have confessed long ago. At the end, he felt Father Val's hands on his head and heard him whisper the words of forgiveness before getting back to his feet.

"I get the feeling that isn't all," Father Val said softly.

"No, but for this I want your advice, not the priest's," Evan told him, hoping Father Val would understand. "There's someone I think I'm in love with. The problem is that I've never told him and don't know how he feels about me, and now that I'm leaving, I'm not sure what I should do. Heck, Father Val, I don't even know if he's gay."

Father Val nodded his head slowly. "Evan, you're eighteen years old. I know these things seem really big and important now, but you have so much of your life ahead of you. Things might and will change as both of you grow. My guidance is to not tell him and leave things as they are. I know in my heart that if this is meant to be, you and Clay will find your way back to one another."

Evan gasped, but Father Val simply patted him on the shoulder. "I'm a priest, but that doesn't mean I don't have eyes. I was in love once myself when I was your age. I know how it feels, but it changed for me, and it will probably change for you. You have a lot of living and a lot of life ahead of you. Experience it, enjoy it. You'll meet a lot of people and learn more things than you can imagine now." Evan felt Father Val lightly squeeze his shoulder before dropping his hand, breathing out a sigh. "You have a life to get on with, so I think it's time you get ready to graduate."

Evan agreed silently, walking toward the door. "I'll see you in a little while," Evan said as he forced a smile before opening the door. Closing it behind him, he found himself really smiling, his heart and spirit light as he walked back toward the dorm.

"Evan!" He didn't recognize the voice right away. Turning around, he saw Dex and his parents walking in his direction, with Dex's mother hurrying ahead of the rest. Then he was being hugged tightly. "Today's a big day for you." Without waiting for him, she led the group toward the dorm. "What are you waiting for?" Evan looked to Dex and found him looking back at him equally confused. "Do you think I'm going to let either of you graduate without making sure you're properly dressed? I don't think so." She turned and continued toward the dorm. "Boys," she called, and both of them found themselves snapping to, much to the delight of everyone around them.

Twenty minutes later, Mrs. Dexter—Dex's real first name was Myron, so no wonder he went by Dex—had them in their graduation gowns and was checking over every last detail in Evan's room. Even Clay was getting the treatment, when a knock briefly sounded on the door.

"Marilyn, can I speak with Evan for a minute?" Dex's father said as he stepped inside.

"Of course, we're done here, anyway. I'll meet you outside." With a final swirl of Chanel, she left the room, winking at Evan for some strange reason on her way out, with everyone else right behind her.

"Son, when Dex told me a while ago how you helped with the design of the school's network, I didn't quite believe it. But I just met your mathematics instructor, and he assured me that it was true. How a high school student could do that is beyond me, but they have all assured me that it's true."

"Numbers sort of speak to me, sir," Evan said nervously.

"Obviously. I'm here because I'd like to offer you a job for the summer as an intern in our IT department. Dex said you weren't sure what you were going to do after graduation. I also contacted some friends of mine in certain admissions offices as well as at certain professional societies, and there will be some scholarship money coming your way—enough that you should be able to attend the college of your choice, and during the summers you'll have a job."

Evan's head swam. "I don't understand."

"Son, many years ago, I attended St. Bart's just like Dex, and I hope his son will as well. Part of the experience is not just the education but making friends who stay with you for the rest of your life. I was the best man at my roommate's wedding, and last year he and his wife joined Marilyn and me on a cruise to the Bahamas. The relationships you make here can last a lifetime, like brothers. And we help our brothers."

Evan found himself completely speechless.

"In case you're wondering, this isn't charity. You earned this through your hard work and potential. I just brought you to the attention of people who can help." After a pat on the shoulder, Mr. Dexter opened the door and Dex and Clay almost fell into the room.

"Listen at doors much?" Evan said with a smile as his two friends celebrated his good fortune along with him. "Well, it looks like I'm going to college after all!" Evan shouted as he bounced on his heels.

"Don't be late, boys," Mr. Dexter said. "Graduation mass starts in ten minutes." He closed the door, and all of them whooped to beat the band.

"We've come so close to telling you for a week now," Dex said as they calmed down. "But Dad wanted to tell you himself."

Getting their caps and making sure their gowns were straight, the three of them walked out into the hall, joined almost immediately by Pete, Wilbur, and Patrick. All of them walked together toward the designated meeting area in one of the classrooms, where they lined up and excitedly waited for the ceremony to begin.

Music drifted in through the open window, and slowly they made their way out of the building, along the sidewalk, and into the chapel where they proceeded down the center aisle to the pews in front. Father Val looked serene in his flowing robes standing next to the bishop with his staff and embroidered miter. After mass, they moved to the auditorium for Baccalaureate and finally the graduation itself. Evan didn't remember too much of the ceremony, his mind still trying to process the news from Mr. Dexter. Looking around him at everyone gathered, his friends, and the instructors, he knew he was blessed, truly blessed, to have been a part of this place and the people in it. Shifting his gaze, he saw Father Valentin smiling back at him.

The speakers gave their presentations, and one by one each of his classmates and friends walked up the steps and across the stage to receive their diplomas and shake hands with both Father Val and the bishop before stepping off and sitting down. At the end of the ceremony, instead of throwing their hats in the air, the band began to play, and everyone stood, singing the school hymn just like at the end of every daily mass. Then, in a wave of hugs and smiles, everyone made their way to their cars. Some were going home already, while others, like him, Clay, and Dex, all went to dinner with parents for a huge celebration before returning to the school for one last night.

Full to bursting, the three of them climbed out of the car, half walking, half waddling toward the door of the dorm. "We'll be back at nine tomorrow morning to take you boys to breakfast," Mrs. Dexter said with a wave before her window slid up and the car pulled out of the parking lot.

"I can't believe your mom and dad offered me a room at their house for the summer," Evan said to Dex, wondering how he'd make it through a whole summer in that huge house. By the fall, he'd be truly spoiled.

"It's no problem. Mom loves having people in the house, and the place is so big. Besides," Dex said, turning to Clay, "when you come to visit, the three of us can go sailing. It'll be great." Dex grinned excitedly, and Evan could barely keep himself under control. Once again, everything in his life seemed to have changed in a day. That morning, he'd been wondering what he was going to do after graduation, where he was going to live, having completely given up on being able to go to college, and now, he was going to bed with scholarships, a summer job, and a place to live. Without thinking, he grabbed Dex and pulled him into a crushing hug before releasing him and doing the same thing to Clay. It took his body only a split second before he felt Clay's heat through his clothes, and his body reacted instantly. It took a few seconds more before he realized his errant cock was rubbing against Clay's hip, and his friend had to have felt it.

Jumping back a little too quickly, he looked at Clay to see if he'd noticed, but Clay's face betrayed nothing. Getting hold of himself, Evan plastered a smile back on his face and continued walking toward the dorm, beating himself up as he walked. He couldn't let on how he felt. Right now, his fantasies about Clay were just that, and they were all he had. Evan could live with that, but what he couldn't bear was the thought of Clay's rejection. As long as he had his dreams, he had some hope.

"You guys up for a pig-out in my room?" Dex asked once the door closed behind them.

Evan knew he could barely eat anything more, and he really wanted to get back to their room with the lights out so he could be alone with his thoughts and feelings for a while. Looking at Clay, he waited for him to answer to see what he wanted to do. "I'm so full I can barely move," Clay said. "I'll see you in the morning."

Dex turned to him, and Evan nodded his agreement, saying, "We'll see you in the morning." He watched as Dex made his way to his room, closing the door behind him, while he and Clay walked to their room.

Evan got his kit from the dresser, walking out to the bathroom. Everything was quiet, since most of the rooms on their floor were empty. Cleaning up quickly, Evan walked back to the room, where he finished getting dressed for bed and slipped under his covers while Clay was in the bathroom. Lights out, he saw the door open, light from the hall shining in until Clay closed the door. Evan heard Clay undressing in the dark, knowing what he'd see if he turned on the light. He'd seen Clay naked enough over the years to vividly remember his honeyed skin, the way his hips formed those divots and lines as they pointed the way to his sex, the way his legs corded when he bent over for something, and of course, the way his butt looked when he changed his underwear. All of that played in his mind as he heard Clay move through the room.

Then he was quiet, no movement at all. Evan couldn't even tell where he was, and he always knew, like his body had a built-in Clay detector, but that wasn't working right now. There was a small creak of the floor and then nothing, and Evan strained his eyes to see in the near total darkness. He thought he could just make out Clay's form standing near the foot of his bed, but he knew that couldn't be right. Evan nearly jumped when he felt a weight settle near the foot of his bed.

"Evan," Clay said softly, his voice rough and deep. "Are you still awake?"

He found himself nodding, not wanting to break whatever spell had come over Clay. He had to be dreaming. Somehow, Evan had to have fallen asleep, because he felt Clay lean closer to him. Holding his breath, he waited to see what would happen, and the weight kept shifting, coming closer. Evan could hear his own breathing echoing in his head. "Clay," he sighed softly and then felt hot breath on his face. Closing his eyes, Evan parted his lips and then felt Clay's touch them ever so lightly. He didn't dare move, and then he felt Clay deepen the kiss slightly. Only then did he allow himself the hope that this was real, that though he'd imagined this so much, his brain wasn't playing tricks on him.

"Ev," he heard Clay whisper, "is this okay?"

Is this okay? He wanted to shout for the world that this was extra-super-especially okay. His mouth dry, Evan swallowed and tried to speak, but it was like he'd been struck mute. Raising his hand, he slipped it behind Clay's neck, gently bringing their lips together once again. He wanted this so badly, had for years, and up till now, he'd had no idea that Clay had wanted him too. "Clay," he said softly, moving his lips away. "We shouldn't... I mean *I* shouldn't...."

Evan felt Clay stiffen above him. "Oh, okay." Evan felt Clay's weight start to lift off the bed, and his hand made a grab for Clay's arm.

"I didn't mean that." Evan held on to that arm like it was a lifeline to everything he'd ever dreamed about in his whole life. "I'm not good enough for you. You should, no, you deserve better than me."

Clay's retreat halted, and Evan could feel him looking down at him. "Why? Why wouldn't you be good enough for me? I know there's something you're afraid of. I can see it whenever anyone asks about your life before you came to St. Bart's."

Damn that man is going to make a great lawyer, Evan thought.

"I don't understand what could be so bad that you'd keep it from me, from your friends, all this time."

"I know you don't," Evan responded, and he gently tugged Clay back toward him, afraid to completely let go or Clay would slip away from him forever. It would happen soon enough tomorrow, but he didn't want it to happen any sooner than it had to. "And it's hard for me to talk about, but trust me. I'm not good enough for you."

Evan felt Clay's weight shift, and for a second he thought Clay was going to pull away, but slowly he felt the other man move closer. "Why don't you let me decide for myself?" Clay moved even closer, settling right next to him, so close he could feel his breathing and smell the spicy scent of his skin.

Evan swallowed. "My parents died months before I came to St. Bart's."

"I remember the day you got here. You looked so scared, like you'd come from a completely different world," Clay said, and Evan could hear the smile in his voice.

"I did, Clay. My folks didn't have much, and when they died in an accident, I found I didn't have anything. A few days later, I was taken out of our tiny apartment and placed with a bunch of strangers. I think they tried to take care of me, but I really can't remember much about them now, except that they weren't my parents or anything. The county had some sort of funeral for my mom and dad, and after that, my foster parents took me home. I didn't talk to anyone for days, and I barely remember eating. All I really remember is wishing the accident had taken me with them."

"Are they the ones that sent you here?" Evan felt Clay move closer to him, and he moved over on the bed to give him room, half expecting him to get up and leave at any second. He kept telling himself that Clay had stood by him before and he would again, but this was so very different.

"No, I ran away, convinced they hated me. I think at the time I just hated the entire world. I thought I could be happier on my own, but I found out otherwise. A few days later, all the money I had in the world was gone. I hadn't eaten much and had no place to live. I saw some other boys standing on street corners and saw them getting into cars. Slowly I approached one of them. A car pulled up, and a man motioned me over. He actually offered me money to take a ride with him." Evan stopped, not really wanting to talk about it anymore. "I spent the next few months going with strange men for food and maybe a place to sleep. Sometimes if I was lucky, they would let me sleep over, and I could clean up and get warm." Evan grew quiet, listening for some reaction from Clay.

"That was where Father Val found me, on the streets. He offered me breakfast and then a place here." Evan thought he was going to cry all of a sudden. "He saved me, Clay." Evan let himself go silent, listening to the sound of Clay's breathing, expecting him to get up and go to his own bed, but he didn't. Clay didn't move at all.

"Is that why you always stood back?"

"Yes. Even though I was here, I guess I thought I probably shouldn't be."

"Yes, you should." Evan felt Clay clutch his hand, entwining their fingers together. "You belong here just as much as the rest of us." Evan felt Clay lean toward him again, finding his lips, the coolness of the room caressing him as Clay lifted the bedding. Clay's skin next to his felt better, smoother, hotter than anything he'd ever imagined. Clay's weight shifted slightly on the bed, and Evan felt him on top, pressing him into the mattress, lips demanding, hot and hard. He could feel Clay's cock against his through their thin layers of cotton. Evan was almost afraid to touch, to do anything that would make Clay stop. But then in the near darkness, Clay was so close that Evan saw the passion for him in Clay's eyes and Evan gasped quietly in surprise. He felt Clay's hand slide down his body, leaving behind trails of burning skin that ached for more. Fingers slid beneath the elastic of his underwear, sliding it down, and then Clay's slipped away, both of them groaning softly as their cocks touched for the very first time.

Evan heard himself sigh softly at the touch, and Clay tugged him closer, kissing harder, letting him know that he wanted the same things Evan did and that what Evan wanted was all right. Letting his hands rove, Evan slowly traced them down Clay's spine and over his butt, fingers splaying against the warm, soft skin. He wanted to feel everything at the same time, and suddenly his hands acted like they had a mind of their own, roaming all over Clay's body as they continued kissing with such intensity he could barely think. Thankfully, he didn't have to. His hands and body knew what they wanted and had no qualms about taking it.

One of Clay's legs slipped between his, a knee sliding back and forth along his leg. The touch nearly had him delirious with pleasure. It seemed as though everything Clay did nearly sent him over the edge and made him want more all at the same time. Clay felt like a drug that he'd denied himself for so long, and he simply couldn't get enough.

"Clay," Evan cried out softly, arching his back as his friend's lips fell away from his, kissing down his skin, tongue sliding around a nipple. In order to keep from crying out even more, Evan buried his face against Clay's shoulder, the flavor of his skin bursting on his tongue. Evan felt his eyes widen, and he had to muffle himself as Clay continued using his lips and tongue on his skin. He wanted more, damn, he needed more, and his entire being threatened to cry out.

Then everything stopped, and Evan blinked into the darkness when he felt Clay lift himself away. Bedding flew away in a rush of cool air, and then Clay's lips were back, hands, too, touching and kissing trails down his stomach. Evan held his breath as Clay's cheek slid against his cock, stomach clenching as he tried to will Clay to do more. "I'm not sure what to do," Clay admitted softly.

Evan smiled to himself and used his hands to guide Clay's face back up to his, where he kissed him once again. "Whatever you want to; you can't do anything wrong."

Evan slipped from beneath Clay, helping him settle on the bed before kissing him once again and letting his own lips roam over Clay's body. He tasted like manly heaven, and Evan determined that he was going to taste everything he could. His tongue swirled around a nipple, his fingers plucking the small buds until Clay writhed on the bed, a hand between his teeth to keep from crying out. Evan tasted Clay's neck, licking slowly over his throat before sliding his hand down the center of his chest, over the small patch of soft hair between his pecs before continuing. Clay laughed lightly when Evan swirled his tongue around his belly button and moaned softly when he teased the small of his hip. Clay stilled completely when Evan's tongue touched him for the first time, sliding all along his length. "Have you ever done this before?" Evan asked quietly.

"No," Clay whined, his voice breaking as Evan swiped his tongue just under the head before sliding his lips along the quaking shaft, Clay thrusting slightly with his hips.

Opening his mouth, Evan sank his lips over Clay, hearing his muffled moan and a quiet plea for more. Slowly he sucked more and more of the shaft, bobbing his head lightly until Clay rocked in rhythm with him. Evan knew Clay couldn't last very long. This was so new for him, the sensations had to be overwhelming. Taking him as deep as he dared, he felt Clay throb against his tongue before making an almost strangled noise and coating Evan's tongue with his release. Evan took everything, savoring the flavor that was uniquely Clay, his Clay. Slipping his lips away, Evan brought their mouths together, sharing Clay's own flavor with him as he rubbed against Clay's skin. Seconds later, Evan felt his body tighten, his own climax building. Holding tight to Clay, muffling his cry against Clay's skin, Evan clamped his eyes closed and came.

Opening his eyes, he could see little more, but slowly Evan began to move. The first thing he did was unclamp his teeth from where he'd bitten Clay's shoulder. Reaching to the small light near his bed, Evan turned it on, staring down into Clay's dark eyes. He wanted to see him. He could no longer guess what he'd been feeling and had to actually see Clay's reaction to what they'd done. Would he be embarrassed or upset? Evan didn't know, but he needed to.

Clay looked... amazing, eyes half-lidded, mouth partly open, chest still rising in exaggerated post-exertion heaves. As he watched, Clay's eyes opened wider and he smiled, a big, full smile that eased Evan's worries and warmed his heart. "Why tonight, Clay?" Evan asked softly, reaching to the floor by the side of the bed, cleaning them off with a T-shirt before settling back on the mattress. "Why did you wait till tonight?"

"I wasn't sure you really wanted me that way. I've watched you for months, and you never made any sort of move. I guess I figured I wasn't your type or something." Clay smirked a little. "Guess I was wrong."

Evan smacked him lightly on the shoulder. "Ya think? You've known I was gay for dang near two years, and you never said anything about you. How was I supposed to know? You never said anything or looked at me any different. I can't read your mind," Evan huffed, realizing all his fantasies had come true, and they could have had this a long time ago. "You were my friend, my best friend, and I wasn't going to ruin that by making a pass at you or something. I mean, I was always afraid it would ruin things."

"I was scared you didn't like me that way." Clay smiled and then began to laugh. "We're a pair of real dopes aren't we?"

"Yeah," Evan said, joining him, "I guess we are." Reaching across Clay, Evan turned off the light, settling on the bed, his arm wrapped around Clay, head on his shoulder. "What do we do now?" he asked before groaning. "God, I sound like one of those characters in one of those movies your mom made us watch last summer, remember?"

"Yeah, Mom's big on the chick flicks," Clay replied, and Evan felt the chuckle ripple through his chest before he stilled and became quiet. "I don't know. I've already been accepted to Notre Dame. I could apply and go to the same college you do. That way we could be together. Maybe we could be roommates and stuff, just like we were here."

Evan felt his heart speed up at the possibility. "I was thinking of UW Madison. We could both go there," he started excitedly and then stopped himself. "You can't do that," he said softly, rolling onto his side so he could face Clay even though he could barely see him. "It wouldn't be fair to you. Notre Dame's where your dad went, and it's what you've dreamed of for so long. I can't ask you to give that up." Evan rested his head back against Clay's skin, breathing his scent deep so he could remember it. "You're going to be a great lawyer, and you'll help a lot of people. You can't throw that away."

Clay shifted, and Evan felt himself being pulled close. "If you don't want me, just say so."

"Clay." Evan had everything he'd ever wanted, and Clay was willing to stay with him. "It's not that at all." Evan realized Father Val had been right. He couldn't be selfish and hold Clay back— he'd never forgive himself if things didn't work out. "Father Val told me today when I talked to him that we were young and had a lot of growing to do."

"We." He felt Clay stiffen with tension.

"Yeah. I told him I was in love with someone and didn't know how to tell him." Evan shifted slightly. "He told me that if we were meant to be together, we'd find a way back to one another. He said we need to experience life, and I think he's right."

"You're in love with me?" Clay asked very softly.

"Yes. I have been for almost as long as I can remember." Evan huffed slightly, wondering if he was doing the right thing telling him this. "But Clay, you're going to a great college that will set you up to be a great lawyer. You'll have opportunities there that you can't other places. I can't let you give that up, just like I don't know what I'd do if I couldn't be around numbers and computers. We'll see each other, I know we will. You'll visit me at Dex's this summer, and we can visit each other in college." Evan could hardly believe he was saying this, not after getting everything he wanted, and he almost shut his mouth and let Clay do whatever he wanted so they could be together. It was what he wanted as well, but it wouldn't be fair, to either of them. Swallowing hard, Evan curled as close to Clay as he could. "We're not kids anymore, and we need to grow up. You need and deserve every opportunity you can get."

"So do you," Clay echoed softly. "So you're saying this is it?"

"God, I hope not," Evan whispered, "but I won't let you throw away your future because of me. I'd never forgive myself, and you'd probably come to hate me for it. I do love you, Clay, more than I've ever loved anyone." Evan felt tears well in his eyes, and he thought of the small amount of time they had left—just tonight. Sure, they'd see each other again, but life would change them; he knew that. He'd seen it in himself. Evan only hoped that Father Val was right, that if they were meant to be together, they would find their way back to each other somehow.

Chapter 4

EVAN woke, stretching slightly in the darkness before curling under the covers in his bed. His own bed in his own tiny apartment, but it was his. The little furniture he had he'd bought over time, but it was all his, as was the small used car that sat outside in his parking space. Closing his eyes again, Evan let his drowsy mind wander, and as usual, it settled on memories of Clay and their one night together. The intervening years had dulled its sharpness, but his mind had also embellished it and built on it. Sliding a hand down his chest, he took himself in hand, stroking lightly, fingers teasing. As always, he imagined that it was Clay touching him the way he'd done that last night at St. Bart's.

He had seen Clay a number of times since their high school graduation. That first summer, Clay had come to visit at Dex's parents, and the three of them had such fun for a few days until Clay had to return to his summer job. They hadn't gotten much time alone, and while they'd kissed and things, they hadn't felt comfortable doing anything else, not with Dex's mother around. After that visit, Evan had worked. Mr. and Mrs. Dexter were indeed kind enough to let him stay with them, so he worked hard, learning everything he could.

In the fall, classes started, and Evan had thrown himself into his studies. He'd made friends, and they were nice enough, but none of them seemed like the guys he knew at St. Bart's. They weren't quite as close or special for some reason. He'd tried to visit Clay at Notre Dame once, but there was no way he could afford the transportation. Clay had visited once in their first year of college, but after that, they'd seemed to drift apart a little. Evan knew it was probably to be expected, but they did e-mail and Facebook to keep in touch, though even that got to be less and less.

In his junior year of college, Evan somehow attracted the attention of a very sexy guy in his quantitative methods class who actually asked him out for coffee. Evan of course demurred, but Kevin was persistent, and eventually Evan met him for coffee, then dinner, a movie, and eventually a kiss. His first kiss that wasn't from Clay—and he liked it, so they did it again. Soon, he was meeting Kevin on a regular basis, and Evan eventually realized he had a boyfriend, at least for a few months until Kevin moved on, or did Evan lose interest? He was never really sure, not that it mattered, not really, because a month or so later, he met Danis, a huge, blond man with plenty of energy who wiped all memory of Kevin away. Danis was something else, but he didn't last very long either. Through the rest of his junior and senior years, Evan had a few additional boyfriends, but none of them lasted very long. Evan knew why. As time went on, they all wanted more and more of Evan's time, but his studies always came first. At graduation, it paid off when he was offered a teaching position at a private high school in a suburb of Milwaukee.

In his junior year, Evan had realized that what he wanted to do was teach mathematics. He wanted to pass his knowledge on to others and to help make sure that what Brother Renier had done to him wouldn't happen to anyone else. So after graduation, he moved to his small downtown apartment and learned how to take care of himself.

His first year of teaching was hard, rewarding, gratifying, and completely exhausting, and he loved every minute of it. The students were good kids who by and large wanted to learn. If they didn't, they learned very quickly not to take Evan's classes, because he worked his students hard, and he was very proud to say they gave him everything he expected and more.

Throughout all the intervening years, the people who kept faithful contact were Dex and Frankie. Dex seemed to be the one who stayed plugged in with everyone's life and what they were doing, while Frankie was just great fun to talk to and be around whenever they could get together. He often missed the days playing with the guys on the lawn, and a few weeks earlier, when he last talked with Frankie, he asked him if he still had that blasted helicopter. They'd both laughed when Frankie told him it made it through the next school year, but on the last day of school, it had crashed into one of the apple trees in the orchard. "It gave its all," Frankie had said.

The alarm sounding broke through Evan's memories, and he realized he was still lying in the bed with his hand on himself, but nothing was happening. Not that it really mattered. The memories of his friends, the best friends he'd ever had, were definitely worth missing a jack-off session for. Shutting off the buzzing, he climbed out from under the covers and made his way to his dinky bathroom. After shaving and cleaning up, he started the shower and then stepped under the warm spray, hoping it would help wake him up. At least today he didn't have classes to teach, but since it was parents' day, he still had to be on and ready for just about anything.

Soaping himself up, Evan's hands roamed over his skin and over his length as Clay popped into his mind once again. Over the years, Evan had wondered why Clay, or his memories of Clay, seemed to have such a powerful hold on him, and the best answer he could come up with was that he didn't honestly know—they just did. Giving in to them, he let his mind conjure up the feel of Clay's skin against his and the way he'd touched him. He vividly remembered the way he'd tasted and longed to taste him again. As his memories took over, Evan let himself float with them, stroking and snapping his hips as the imaginary Clay did unimaginable things to him. Evan felt his legs begin to shake as his mind's Clay went down on his knees, taking him into his mouth. Squeezing himself tightly, Evan shot hard, his mind floating on endorphins before the chilling water reminded him he better get moving before it turned completely cold. Rinsing off quickly, Evan turned off the water and stepped out. Drying hurriedly, he walked into this bedroom and got dressed for work.

Leaving the apartment, Evan walked to his parked car. It wasn't new, but it was very reliable. Mr. Dexter had sold it to him when he'd gotten his first job, and Evan thought he'd quoted him a ridiculously low price, but the look on Mr. Dexter's face told him it would be insulting to question it, so he didn't. Opening the door to his red Volvo coupe, Evan slid behind the wheel, starting the engine before beginning the drive to school. The ride to work took him over half an hour, partly because of traffic as well as distance. The one thing Evan was grateful for was that most of the traffic was going the other way. As he got out of town, houses fell away and the landscape became lush, the leaves changing to their fall reds and yellows. Pulling into the parking lot, he waved as a few other teachers arrived, but didn't stay to talk; he had plenty to do.

The school had a policy that required at least one parent of each student to meet their child's teachers. This was their way of trying to ensure that the often wealthy parents got involved with the school as well as their kids' education. Evan had his doubts regarding how effective it was, but kept them to himself. Quietly opening the door, Evan walked through the building, his footsteps echoing off gleaming floors and sparkling lockers. Here, everything was shiny and new.

Unlocking the door to his room, he turned on the lights and flopped his bag onto his desk before making a detailed inspection of the classroom. As he'd found out last year, Arthur Pinkus, the director of the school, required that every room look its absolute best for the parental visits. "After all, they were the ones who wrote the checks," he'd actually said. Walking through the room, he inspected everything before opening the door to the adjacent computer lab. Booting up the machines, he got them logged on and ready.

"Everything okay?" he heard Arthur ask as he stuck his head in.

"Seems to be. Do you see anything you'd like changed?" Evan asked and saw the director look around.

"Looks good," he said with a smile before turning, and Evan heard his footsteps retreat. Finishing his preparations, he pulled his papers out of his bag, making sure he had examples of each student's work easily at hand. He had some stellar students, but he also had ones who were struggling, and Evan suspected they were being pushed into classes they weren't quite ready for. He needed to be ready.

"Hello." A man poked his head around the corner of the doorway. "Are you Mr. Donaldson?" The rest of him followed when Evan nodded.

"Please come in."

A man about Evan's age with wavy blond hair and a huge, warm smile walked into the room, and Evan found himself wondering how this man could possibly be the parent of one of his students—he was way too young. "I know," he said, looking at himself. "There's no way I'm a parent of one of your students. I'm Leonard Fetzer; my niece Helene is in your advanced algebra class. My older brother and his"—he made a show of counting on his fingers—"third wife, I guess it is, are in Switzerland, and I graciously volunteered to stand in for Harry today." He looked all around. "It hasn't changed at all since I was here."

"Then you must have had Mr. Wurlitzer?" Evan inquired as he approached the handsome man. "He retired a few years ago. This is my second year teaching at Kohler." Evan found himself smiling like a fool at the man, and to his surprise, Leonard kept smiling back.

"Umm, I should show you some of Helene's work," Evan said, silently berating himself for getting distracted. He must have come off as some sort of idiot or something. "She's a great student when she applies herself," Evan began as he pulled out examples of Helene's work. "Some days she's diligent and her work is perfect, and others she's distracted. Her distractions definitely show in her work." Evan handed Leonard copies of both Helene's good and less-than-stellar work. "I wish I could figure out what makes her tick because she has amazing potential, but she only seems to use it part of the time."

Leonard examined the work and handed the papers back to Evan. "I'm afraid, Mr. Donaldson, that she's feeling the effects of my brother's, shall we say, *exuberant* lifestyle. He and Helene's stepmother have been away in the last year more than they've been home, and my niece has been spending a lot of time with her mother." Leonard shook his head. "My brother has singular taste in women: big boobs and empty heads. Unfortunately, that includes Helene's mother. I spend as much time as I can with her, but I'm not her father, and I think that's what she wants and needs."

Evan nodded slowly. He'd seen it plenty over the last year. "Sometimes these kids have everything except the one thing they need most." Evan snapped his head, looking at Leonard, suddenly realizing he'd said that out loud and that he came off as completely sanctimonious.

Leonard's eyes blazed for just a second. "Do you know what it's like to have an absent father?" Leonard asked.

"Yes. My parents died when I was a teenager. I know some of what Helene's going through," Evan answered, and saw Leonard's expression soften. "She's a teenage girl, and she desperately needs her parents right now," Evan added, wondering what he could do to help her. "Would you like to see some more of her work? She's amazing with computers." Evan moved toward the lab and brought up one of Helene's applications. "She's very interested in fashion and developed formulas to help people pick out clothing based upon a number of factors including height, weight, and skin tone. She developed numerical values for the answers and the formulas to apply them. She has more work to do, though it'll never be perfect because of the strictly visual elements." Evan stood back and let Leonard look at her work.

Hearing other people walk into the other room, Evan excused himself and introduced himself to the other parents, checking his files for examples of their children's work. They looked it over briefly before thanking him and making a quick review of the classroom and exiting again. He'd found out a lot of the visits would be that way, like an unpleasant task they had to perform.

"I should let you meet with the others," Leonard said from behind him before extending his hand. "It was a pleasure to meet you." They shook hands, and then Evan watched him go, touching his tingling fingers as he wondered if Leonard had purposely held his hand a little too long. Other parents entered his room, and Evan knocked himself out of his thoughts as he answered their questions and gave tours of the room while explaining what their son or daughter had been doing.

A few hours passed, and Evan lost track of the number of parents he'd met and talked to, but the first meeting of the day stayed fresh in his mind, especially that smile. "Knock, knock," Evan heard someone say from the door during a lull in the visits, and Evan didn't try to stop his smile as he saw Leonard walk into the room. "I wanted to thank you for your honesty about Helene. Her other teachers all talked about what a wonderful girl she was, and it was only after I pressured them that I got the same information you gave me right away."

Evan felt himself redden. "They're more diplomatic than I am."

Leonard didn't look as though he was buying the explanation, but now wasn't the time for a philosophical discussion of education. Leonard looked toward the door. "Helene told me I had to meet with you first. It seems you've made quite an impression on my niece regardless of her performance."

"Oh?" Evan wondered just what the impression was. He'd had students with crushes on him, but he hadn't seen anything like that from Helene.

"Yeah, she told me I had to meet her cute algebra teacher," Leonard said softly. "I'm probably being a little forward, but I've learned that you don't get anything unless you're willing to go for it. So, Helene was sort of playing matchmaker, if you get my meaning." Leonard smiled, his eyes crinkling just a little at the corners, and said, "And I was wondering if you might be interested in dinner."

"Helene?" Evan tried to say something, but that was the only thing that came out. He'd tried very hard not to give any indication he was gay to any of his students, or fellow teachers, for that matter. "She?"

Leonard stepped back slightly. "Sorry," he said, holding up his hands. "I didn't mean to be insulting or anything."

"You weren't," Evan corrected with a smile. "I thought I was pretty good at keeping that portion of my life out of the classroom, and now it seems my students seem to know my preferences."

"I don't think your students know in general. Helene is quite perceptive, and she probably picked up on you because she and I have spent a lot of time together. So, are you interested—in dinner, I mean?" Other parents coming in the door forced Evan to make a decision. Reaching into his bag, he pulled out a card, scrawling his cell number on it. He handed the card to Leonard, giving him a quick nod before turning his attention to the parents looking around his classroom. With a spring in his step, he walked over, introducing himself.

Lunch consisted of a snatched few minutes with a sandwich behind his desk between bouts of visiting parents. So far it had been a very interesting and productive morning. He'd met the parents of some of his most gifted students. He'd also met the pushiest father ever, bound and determined that his son was going to be the best, even when he was struggling. And of course, he'd gotten a date, and with a very handsome man at that. He knew he needed to be careful, because the man was the uncle of one of his students, but as long as it didn't enter the classroom, it should be fine.

Evan put his sandwich on top of his brown bag when his phone vibrated in his pocket. Normally, he took no phone calls during the day, but since he didn't have students in the room, he'd left his phone in his pocket. "Hi, Dex, how are you?" Evan asked after he'd checked the ID of the caller.

"Good. I know it's during the day, and I was expecting to leave a message. Can you talk a minute?"

Evan glanced out into the hall, but it appeared empty. "Sure, I have a few minutes."

"I just got a call from Frankie, and he said that Clay's getting married."

Evan swallowed and almost dropped the phone. "Clay?"

"Yeah. Frankie said he's marrying someone he met in law school. They've reportedly been dating off and on for a while, and now that he's about to graduate, he decided to take the plunge. Frankie said he's gotten an offer from one of the big firms in Milwaukee. You hadn't heard?"

"No," Evan answered definitely feeling hurt.

"Guess he hadn't gotten around to calling you yet," Dex said, still excited. Somehow Evan doubted that Clay would get around to calling him.

"Dex, I have to go. Today's parents' day and there are some standing outside my door," he lied. "I'll call you later."

"Sure," Dex said happily. "You doing anything for the holidays? Mom wanted me to pass one of her special invitations on to you, and you know what that means...."

Evan chuckled through his anxiety. "I do. Tell her I wouldn't miss it for the world."

"I will," Dex answered and said goodbye before hanging up. Shoving his phone into his pocket, Evan stared at the back wall of his classroom, lunch forgotten. *Clay getting married?* That was the last thing he ever expected. After that night they'd spent together, Evan honestly figured Clay was gay. "Damn," he whispered under his breath. *Was that night just some experiment on Clay's part?* It had meant a lot to Evan, but it obviously meant a hell of a lot less to Clay. Standing up, Evan wandered through the empty classroom. He'd held the memory of Clay and him together as nearly sacred for all these years, a special memory he'd shared with no one, ever. When relationships ended and boyfriends left, he always held on to that one night he'd had with Clay. *Was it all a lie? Was Evan simply some experiment of Clay's while he figured out what he wanted?* Closing his eyes, Evan tried to remember back to that night to pull up some clue, but nothing new came forward. Time had dulled the memories, and now it almost felt as though this had soiled it somehow.

"Mr. Donaldson." He heard a woman's voice behind him. "Are you all right?"

Evan schooled his face as best he could. "Yes, please come in," he said as the impeccably dressed lady glided toward him, introducing herself as Elaina Fordham, almost regally, before lowering herself into one of the chairs before they began reviewing her son's work. By the time they were done, Elaina had surprised Evan by making him laugh, and she'd found out that her son was one of his brightest students, nearly a full year ahead of his classmates.

"I always dress like this when I come here," she said, leaning close. "You never know when one of the damned bitches will see you, and there's no way I'm going to be upstaged by any of them." Evan had laughed out loud when she let down her façade, revealing an accent that sounded remarkably like his own rather than the polished one she'd used when she'd entered. "They live in their big houses on borrowed money, trying to keep up appearances, and look down on me because I actually worked for my money." She lifted her head, and Evan smiled. This woman reminded him of the Molly Brown character in *Titanic*. Her phone rang in her purse, and she excused herself, briefly taking the call before saying goodbye. Evan watched her go, gliding down the hallway as though she were a queen, and Evan smiled to himself. If nothing else, she'd pushed his maudlin thoughts away. Other parents came and went for the rest of the afternoon, and Evan forced his mind onto his work, keeping himself occupied until it was time to pack up and go home.

The drive took a while, like it usually did in the evenings, and his phone buzzed just as Evan pulled into his parking space. It was a number he didn't recognize. "I didn't call too early, did I? It's Leonard, from this morning."

Evan found himself smiling. "No, I was just getting home." Opening the car door, he got out, careful of the other cars as he closed his door. "I wasn't sure you were going to call." Evan opened the trunk, pulling out his bag as he talked.

"Well, I did. It's not often I meet a smart, good-looking man." Evan felt himself redden as his cheeks warmed in the cool air. "Anyway, are we still on for dinner?"

"If you're serious, I'd like to have dinner with you." He was a little concerned about dating the relative of a student, but he'd checked the school policies and while it had been explicit about his behavior, his contract hadn't said anything forbidding this type of relationship. There were prohibitions about dating the parents of students, but not their uncles. It was only dinner, after all, and he was sure it would be fun.

"Excellent." He could hear the excitement in Leonard's voice, and he found some of it transferring to himself. "If you tell me where you live, I'll pick you up at six thirty." Evan gave him directions and hung up the phone. This could be good. He'd held on to his memories and fantasies of Clay for far too long. The guys he'd dated before had nearly all looked the same: tall, broad, and dark, like Clay. There had been some exceptions, but not many. Leonard was nothing like Clay, not in the way he looked nor in the way he acted, at least as far as Evan could tell. Maybe this was a good thing, a very good thing. Pulling open the door to his building, Evan found himself whistling softly as he entered the empty elevator, riding up to his floor. Clay was moving on and so would he. There was no shame in that.

Stepping out of the elevator, he hurried to his door, unlocking it before rushing through his small living room to his bedroom. Undressing quickly, he stepped into the shower for a quick rinse before drying himself and rushing to his closet, where he stared trying to figure out what to wear. No matter how much he looked, nothing new or fabulous appeared by magic, so Evan pulled out his best-looking slacks and a nice shirt. He hoped it looked good enough. After dressing, he spritzed on a small amount of cologne before pulling on his socks and shoes. The buzzer near the door sounded, and Evan called down before pressing the button to let Leonard in, telling him the floor. He'd just finished tying his shoes and taking a quick glance in the mirror before a soft knock sounded at the door. Pulling it open, he saw Leonard, dressed impeccably, carrying a bouquet of flowers. "I know it's cliché, but I couldn't arrive empty-handed," Leonard said with a smile before handing them to Evan.

"Thank you." No one had ever given Evan flowers before, and he smiled, closing the door behind his guest, offering him a chair as he hurried to put them in water. "I wasn't expecting these," Evan said from the kitchen as he found a pitcher, running water for the flowers before setting them on the table. "They're beautiful and very thoughtful," Evan commented, still smiling as he walked back into the living room. Leonard was walking around the room and seemed to be taking it all in. "Leonard, are you ready to go, or do we have time for a drink? I have a bottle of wine if you'd like some," Evan offered, not sure whether Leonard was ready to eat already.

"Actually," Leonard said, turning away from a picture of Evan at St. Bart's, "I made seven o'clock reservations, so we should go. And please call me Leo."

Evan returned his smile before following him to the door. Locking it, he waited with Leo for the elevator. Evan didn't know what to say and found himself looking at Leo and everything around him, trying to find some topic of conversation. "Did you always want to be a teacher?" Leo asked, breaking the silence.

"Originally, I wanted to be a mathematician and study mathematics, but in my junior year, I decided to teach." Evan answered. The elevator doors opened and they stepped inside. "It's really rewarding, especially when a student who's been struggling gets one of those 'aha' moments and you get to see when the light goes on. It's really cool. What do you do?"

Leo pressed the button and the door closed. "I'm director of sales at Fetzer Printing. My father runs the company, and I work for him."

"Sounds like you have a lot of responsibility. Is it fun working for family?" The doors slid open and they stepped into the hall.

"Sometimes it can be great, but with my brother out of the country, I need to help pick up the slack," Leo explained as he led them out of the building and up to a midnight blue BMW. Unlocking the door, he waited for Evan to get in before walking to his side of the car and starting the engine. "I hope you like Italian."

"Yes, I do."

Leo pulled out of the parking space and into traffic. "I found this little place that makes their own pasta and sauces, it's really wonderful," Leo explained as they rode. "What else do you do besides teach?"

"I volunteer one night a week, serving food at a homeless shelter. When I was fifteen, my parents died and I found myself living on the streets. I was helped by a kind man who gave me the chance at a real life." Evan looked over at Leo, who to his surprise seemed to be hanging on every word. "Father Val was incredibly kind to me and never asked anything in return, so I give back where I can, sort of as a thank you to him."

"Sounds like you had quite a childhood," Leo commented. "Mine was nothing like that. My dad ran a successful business he inherited from his father, so we had almost everything you could imagine. Mom spoiled us rotten, but Dad insisted we both make something of our lives. I went to business school and my brother went to law school. He's our corporate lawyer, and we both support Dad since he's getting on in years." Leo sighed, but didn't say any more. "Let's talk about something more fun."

"Okay, what do you suggest? I haven't done a lot since I got out of college. I went to the museum a few weeks ago and saw a great exhibit of Chihuly glass. It was amazing."

"I saw that same exhibit, and I saw his installation at the Venetian in Las Vegas a few years ago—his stuff is incredible," Leo added with excitement before finding a parking space. Getting out of the car, Leo waited for him before escorting him into the restaurant, giving his name to the hostess.

"Are you always like this?" Evan asked as they were escorted to their table.

"Like what?"

"I don't know, a gentleman. I mean, no one's ever treated me like this before," Evan said as he sat down.

"Well, they should. You deserve to be treated well," Leo said with a certain fire in his eyes, his hand ghosting over Evan's. The server approached and introduced herself. Leo ordered a bottle of sparkling wine, and the server returned with an ice bucket, uncorking the bottle with a flourish and a pop before pouring them each a glass. She told them about the specials and took their orders before leaving them to talk. "It's always funny when you're out with someone the first time. You never know what to talk about."

"It's been a while since I was on a date or anything," Evan said as he looked into Leo's eyes. "I haven't gone out much since I got out of college."

"What do you do during summer vacation?"

"I spend part of the time with a friend from high school. He and his family sort of took me under their wing. Dex's family has a sailboat, and his mother... well... she mothers me for the entire week. Other than that, I spend the summers teaching remedial reading classes at the public school near the apartment. I'd like to be able to take the time off, but I can't right now. How about you? What do you do for fun?" Evan tried to hold up his end of the conversation, and he found it fun being here with Leo. He seemed easy to talk to, and Evan felt some of his nervousness begin to slip away.

"We boat on Lake Michigan. Dad has a cabin cruiser that we take out. I also play baseball on the company team. During the winter, I work and hibernate till spring," Leo answered with a grin.

"Why don't I believe that? You seem like the kind of guy who needs something to do all the time," Evan teased, taking a sip from his glass.

"Okay, you got me. But maybe I'd like to hibernate if I had someone cute to hibernate with."

Leo's simmering expression went to Evan's toes, warming him with a touch of excitement. Yes, he would like to hibernate all winter curled up next to Leo, making love in front of a fire somewhere. Sure, it was probably a ridiculous notion, but sitting across from him, looking into those smoldering eyes, it seemed like a very real possibility. Their meals arrived, and the server set a bowl of steaming pasta in front of him, the aroma of the rich white sauce wafting to his nose on the steam. A sound of sheer anticipatory pleasure echoed in his throat, and Evan saw Leo's expression darken. "I wonder what it would take to get you to make that sound for me."

Evan's eyes widened as the little shivers he'd been experiencing kicked up a notch. Shifting his legs beneath the table to a more comfortable position, Evan accidentally on purpose dropped his napkin, using the retrieval process to adjust himself, not that it helped in the least. Leo seemed to be pressing all the right buttons, and part of him wanted to inhale the food so they could get on to other things. Taking a deep breath, he retrieved his napkin, placing it back on his lap, seeing Leo smirking at him across the table. "What?" Evan asked looking down at himself.

"You are completely adorable, you know that?" Leo whispered, eyes sparkling across the table, before taking a small bite of his pasta. "It's been a long time since I've met someone like you."

Evan's fork stopped in midair. "Someone like what?" He didn't know what Leo meant, but the connotations weren't flattering.

Leo finished his bite, setting down his fork. "I didn't mean it like that. I meant that most of the men I meet are interested in me for my money or what I can do for them. I had one man who asked me out figuring if he slept with me, I would get my dad to hire him. You're not like that at all."

Evan shook his head. "No. I haven't had much in my life, but what I have I've earned or had the good fortune to have received by the help of very generous, kind people who've treated an orphan like family. If money were all I wanted, I could have sold myself to the highest bidder in the computer industry. Instead, I teach children at a small private high school." Truth be known, Evan's greatest longing was to love and be loved. He didn't need money for that. Evan took a bite of his pasta, the flavors dancing on his tongue.

Leo took another bite and then set down his fork again, his look intense. "If you could have one thing, what would it be?"

Evan opened his mouth to answer, but stopped himself, because the name Clay nearly tripped off the tip of his tongue, and that wasn't fair. Not tonight. That wasn't possible, and holding on to fantasies was simply foolish. So Evan thought for a second. "I think I'd like children. Their love isn't predicated on what you have or what you can buy them. They love you for you." Leo picked up his fork and began eating again, while Evan found himself lost in thought for a few seconds. When he looked up again, he couldn't help grinning. A long piece of pasta hung out of Leo's mouth, and he was sucking it in. "Are you demonstrating or just showing off?"

Leo laughed, quickly reaching for his water. "That was evil," he responded with a smirk, "but very good. You'll have to let me know… later." An undeniable electric zing shot through Evan, and he had to use everything to keep himself from immediately agreeing. He did not go home with anyone on the first date, and he didn't bring people back to his apartment, either. Those days had ended when he went to St. Bart's. Yes, he knew other guys did it, but Evan still equated that behavior with what he'd done on the streets, and he wasn't going back there. He needed to get to know the person before he'd allow himself to get physical.

Evan needed to change the subject. "Do you travel a lot for work?"

"Some. I have three salespeople who work for me, and they travel a lot, but I meet with important clients, and sometimes that requires that I travel. I really don't mind it as long as it isn't too often. My dad's getting older, and I like to be around to help support him." Leo chewed and swallowed. "Don't get me wrong," he continued, "my dad's really with it, but he's started to second-guess some of his decisions."

"It must be nice to work with your dad," Evan commented quietly. "You get to see him every day." A sudden longing came over him. He hadn't really thought of his parents in quite some time, and the longing he'd felt after their deaths had faded. But sometimes…

"You said you lost your parents when you were young," Leo prompted. "That must have been hard."

"It was. For a long time, I wished I'd been with them," Evan answered, not really wanting to talk about it. Why did most conversations seem to come back to that? "But I was lucky," Evan said with a smile, reaching across the table and touching Leo's hand. Leo turned his hand over, his fingers sliding along Evan's. The conversation slipped into a comfortable quiet as they finished eating, each looking into the other's eyes.

"Would you like dessert?" Leo asked when their plates were empty, his voice low and quiet like he didn't want to break the spell that seemed to bind them together.

Evan didn't look away from Leo's dark eyes, shaking his head a little. When the server came, Evan barely noticed her as Leo arranged for the check. Getting up, Evan slipped on his jacket, and Leo held his hand as they walked to the car. That simple gesture was as sweet as any Evan could remember. When they got to the car, Evan didn't want to let go. Leo's hand in his felt nice—warm, and sort of right.

"Would you like to come back to my house for a drink?" Leo asked, but before Evan could answer he continued, "No, I have a better idea." Leo lifted their clasped hands, kissing the back of his before releasing the touch. "Much better." Evan saw Leo's smile and heard the excitement in his voice. Wondering what he was up to, Evan waited for Leo to unlock the car.

Soon they were off again, Leo still grinning as they made their way toward the lake. Leo parked the car near the edge of the park. "Is this where we're headed?" Evan asked, peering out the window at the lighted paths.

"I thought we could go for a walk." Leo said, and Evan nodded, turning back to Leo to give him a smile.

Getting out of the car, Leo chirped it locked and then waited for Evan, leading him down one of the paved paths around the edge of the lawn. "Lake Park was designed by Frederick Law Olmstead, the man who designed Central Park in New York," Leo explained as the path led them around the edge of a large lawn, old-fashioned lantern-style lamps lighting the way. Leo slipped his hand into his as the path entered a wooded area, an old lighthouse standing above them. "I love this place. There are hidden surprises around almost every bend in the path."

Evan didn't say much. This place brought back memories, but they were ones he'd rather stayed forgotten. When he'd been here as a homeless teenager, these bends had represented potential danger where people could hide and where men would take him to….

"Evan, are you okay?" Leo asked in a whisper, stopping their walk. "You're all tense, and your eyes are huge."

"I'm sorry." Evan steadied himself, knowing his reaction was completely irrational. "I'm fine." Evan smiled and felt Leo squeeze his hand before they started walking again. The path wound around another lawn before passing through a wooded area once more. Large lions appeared ahead, and they walked past a seating shelter before another set of crouched lions greeted them at the entrance to an ornate footbridge.

"This is my favorite place in the park," Leo said, walking them to the center. The bridge spanned a ravine with a small road below lined with more of the old-fashioned lamps, their light shining up into the trees, illuminating the sides of the bridge while casting them in shadow. "It's so quiet here, almost like we're not in the city at all."

Evan felt Leo's hand slide out of his as fingers gently caressed his cheek. "You're a special man, Evan Donaldson."

"How do you know that?" Evan asked, knowing the things he'd done in his past. The years had dulled the sensations and the recollections, but he'd never quite been able to let them go, and on a night like this, he wished he could. "We only met today."

"I just know," Leo breathed softly, a palm sliding lightly over his cheek. Evan slid his eyes closed, leaning into the touch almost like a cat, the warm hand on his skin, a tender touch, just what he'd been craving. A second hand joined the first, cradling his face in warmth. Hot breath touched his lips, and Evan didn't move, didn't open his eyes, simply waiting. Lips touched his, moist, soft, and warm, the kiss barely there. Evan leaned forward, intensifying the kiss, letting Leo know it was welcome, wanted, heck—needed. Evan felt Leo's lips pull away, and he opened his eyes, meeting Leo's in the reflected light from below. Gazes locked together, they stared for seconds, hours, Evan had no idea at all. Then he saw Leo move closer, and his eyes slid closed once again as Leo drew him forward, kissing him hard, with an earnest passion he could feel in the kiss and against his hip.

There was no doubt Leo desired him. You couldn't fake the considerable evidence, and Evan nearly went with it. His brain screamed at him to let himself go, let the ardor he felt building within himself take over. When the kiss gentled and Leo backed away, Evan found himself gasping for breath, chest heaving in the cool night air. "Wow," he murmured under his breath, looking into Leo's eyes, seeing that he felt the same thing. Without waiting, Evan slid his arms around Leo's neck, tugging the slightly taller man down. Kissing him hard, Evan felt Leo's lips part. Slipping his tongue past, Evan explored Leo's hot mouth as they surrounded themselves in small moans. Leo tasted heavenly and Evan wanted more.

Sounds from outside their wooded cocoon intruded, and Evan pulled out of the kiss, stepping back, lips tingling as the soft whispers of another couple drifted to them between the trees. Leo's hand slipped back into his, and reluctantly, Evan forced his wobbly legs to carry him off the bridge and along the winding path.

They made a large circle, with their return taking them along the edge of the park, across the street from the stately homes and mansions that called the park their front yard. Evan's heart beat rapidly the entire time, his attention on the feel of Leo's hand in his and the occasional gentle touches. Evan didn't want their walk to end, but the evening air wound its way beneath their jackets, and by the time they reached the car, the chill had made it to his skin. Leo unlocked the car, and Evan slid into the seat as Leo started the engine before pressing buttons on the console. Soon his seat warmed him, the car filling with heat as Leo slowly drove the park road, passing under the bridge where they'd kissed, and without thought, Evan brought a finger to his still tingling lips.

The drive continued along the lake before climbing the hill, Leo turning onto Evan's street and parking in front of his building.

"I know I'd talked about asking you up for a drink, but I think we should take this slower," Leo said softly as the leather seat crunched under his shifting weight. "I'll call you tomorrow, okay?" Evan nodded his answer, swallowing as Leo got closer. "If you agree, I'd like to take you out on Saturday. We could go to the symphony and have dinner." Leo's lips cut off Evan's agreement, but after their kiss, Leo seemed to understand his answer. Opening the car door, Evan got out of the car, then closed the door and walked inside. Waiting in the lobby, he watched Leo pull away before pressing the button to call the elevator.

Unlocking his door, Evan walked inside. He closed the door behind him before flopping onto his sofa, a huge smile on his face. He hadn't been sure what to expect, but he hadn't imagined he'd come home still feeling tingly. Checking the clock, he knew he should go to bed, but he had way too much energy. Turning on the television, he slipped off his shoes, watching whatever was on as he thought about Leo.

His phone vibrated on the coffee table, and Evan picked it up, still smiling, expecting it to be Leo. "Hey," he answered, still grinning.

"Evan is that you?" a familiar voice asked. "It's Clay."

The smile faded a little. "Hey, sorry, I was expecting someone else. How are you doing? I haven't heard from you in a while." Evan played dumb.

"I wanted to call and tell you that I'm getting married." Clay sounded appropriately excited but nothing more, sort of like he was reacting the way he thought he should. But then that could have been Evan's wishful thinking.

"That's great!" Evan mustered up some fake enthusiasm of his own. "Have you set a date?"

"No," Clay answered, "Sheila's still got a year of law school left, so we're going to wait until she graduates and has a job. But I asked her yesterday, and she said yes!"

Evan wanted to ask him all the questions he'd asked himself earlier, but stopped them. That was the past, and it was best left there. "So do you have a job?" He already knew the answer, but there was no need for Clay to know he'd been talking to Dex.

"Yes. As matter of fact I'll be working in Milwaukee for a while and was wondering if you'd like to get together when I get to town. I don't know many people there, and I was hoping we could catch up." Some of the excitement had faded from Clay's voice.

"That'd be great. Neither of us has been very good at keeping in touch, so we have plenty to catch up on." Part of him was excited beyond belief at the thought of Clay being in town, and part of him wished he'd stay away. The man was getting married to a woman, after all. That should have told him plenty. But Clay was also one of his best friends, or he had been, at least.

"I know and I'm sorry about that. School got so busy for both of us, but we can change that now. Ev, you were always one of my best friends, and I miss you, man." For a second, Evan wondered if Clay had been drinking.

"I missed you too." He had, and if Clay wanted to be friends, he could handle that, he thought. They'd been friends for years living together at school, and Evan felt certain he could do it again. He was an adult now with his own life and hopefully someone who liked him and wanted him for him. Yes, it was too early to pin any hopes on Leo, but he'd been out on a date, and he could go on more. "When will you get to town?"

"This weekend. I thought we could get together Saturday evening for a few drinks. We can talk, and you can tell me about this school where you're teaching."

"I can't Saturday. I have a date, but we could get together on Sunday afternoon." He smiled when he thought of Leo.

"Sure, Sunday's good," Clay responded quickly, almost too quickly. "You've got my number now. Why don't you call me later in the week and let me know where you'd like to meet."

"Will Sheila be coming with you?" He wasn't sure he really wanted to meet her, but he wasn't going to shy away from her either.

"No, she can't leave school right now, so it'll be just us guys." He didn't sound too disappointed to Evan, but that was none of his business. The more he thought about it, and he thought about it plenty for most of the day, Evan knew what he'd felt with Clay, and nothing else mattered. Clay couldn't fake what they'd done and how he'd felt. If Clay wanted to marry a woman, that was his business, and he wasn't going to get involved. He'd be his friend, but nothing more. Besides, regardless, he'd have his best friend back. That in itself was good. Who would have thought, a possible boyfriend and his best friend all in one day—that wasn't half bad.

"Cool, I'll call you Friday and let you know where to meet me."

"Thanks, Ev," Clay said, a definite touch of sadness evident in his voice before disconnecting.

Putting the phone on the table, Evan turned off the television. Packing his school bag, he also got his lunch ready so he'd have a few extra minutes before leaving for work. It was late and he had classes in the morning, so he rushed through his evening cleanup, then slipped beneath the covers. Closing his eyes, Evan let his mind wander. Ever since high school, Clay had played a starring role in his fantasies, but tonight, he couldn't see his face. All he knew was how he made him feel.

Chapter 5

SATURDAY, thank God it was Saturday. No students, just a day of peace and quiet. That's what Evan thought, until his phone began ringing almost as soon as he got out of bed. "Hello," Evan answered, still not quite awake, padding to the kitchen for coffee.

"Evan, it's Leo." He sounded strange, and Evan wondered what was going on. "I need to talk to you. Is it okay if I come over?" Evan looked at the clock, wondering what the hell time it was.

"Sure," he answered, instantly on his guard for some reason. "I'll have coffee on."

"Thanks," Leo answered before disconnecting.

Setting the phone down, Evan looked at it, wondering what was going on. In the eighteen months they'd been seeing each other, he'd never gotten a phone call like that from Leo, ever. Instantly his mind began going over what could have happened. His first thought was that something had happened to Leo's father. He hoped everyone was okay. Well, he'd find out soon enough.

A number of things had changed since he'd met Leo. He'd moved into a larger apartment in the same building that had a second bedroom. He used the other room as an office, and it had made life a lot easier having his papers filed and organized rather sorted by piles on the table. With the larger apartment came a nicer bathroom, which he appreciated each and every morning. Cleaning up, Evan padded to his bedroom, pulling on a pair of jeans and a T-shirt before walking to the kitchen to make breakfast. Since Leo was on the way, Evan set two places and began making Leo's favorites: bacon and French toast. He'd started the bacon before whipping the egg mixture and getting the bread ready, when he heard Leo at the door. "It's open," he called as he moved the bacon to the paper towels. "I hope you're hungry," Evan added as he saw Leo step into the kitchen. "What is it?"

"I need to talk to you. It's important." Leo looked really serious, his face and eyes set.

"Okay," Evan said as he turned off the heat, following Leo into the living room and sitting at one edge of the sofa. "What is it you want to talk about? Is everyone all right?"

"That's you, always worried about everyone else." Leo sighed. "Everyone's fine as far as I know. I need to talk to you about something else."

Evan watched as he paced from one side of the room to the other. "Just say it, Leo. Whatever it is, just say it," Evan said forcefully. "Nothing could be as bad as all that."

"Evan, I don't think we should see each other anymore," Leo blurted as he looked anywhere in the room but at Evan. "You're a great guy, but we want different things. You've applied to adopt a child, and the thought of raising kids scares me to death. I know that children are something you want very badly, and I respect that, but it's not something I want."

"Why didn't you say anything before now?" Evan felt as though he were being blindsided. He'd talked about children on their first date, and Leo had never said anything. "You've had plenty of chances."

"At first I thought it was a whim, but then you kept talking about it. I should have said something, but then you went ahead and filled out the applications and even went through all the home visits and got the larger apartment, and I didn't want to pop your bubble. You were happy and excited, while I got more and more afraid. The thought of being a parent scares me to death, and that's just something I don't think I want."

Evan sat staring at the far wall, looking right through Leo. He hadn't seen this coming at all. Not an inkling. As far as he'd known, everything had been fine. They'd gone out for dinner just a few days earlier. Leo had stayed the night, and they'd even made love. "How long have you been thinking about this?" Evan shivered, thinking he'd been sleeping with someone he didn't know at all.

"A while now," Leo answered softly. "I tried to tell you last week, but couldn't."

"You knew this Wednesday when we went out and came back here." Evan felt his anger rising. "You made love to me, and you knew you were going to break up with me! What was I to you? Some plaything?"

"No, you were never that, Evan. I care for you, I always have, and I still do. It's just that we want different things, and I can't be part of what you need right now." He felt Leo's hand touch his cheek. "I meant what I said, you're a sweet man, and you're going to make a great father, but I can't take that journey with you. Not that you've really wanted it to be me."

Evan leapt to his feet. "What is that supposed to mean? I love you, Leo, and I thought we could build a life together. I know you're not interested in that now, but you don't get to make assumptions about what I want and what I don't!" Evan glared at Leo, who simply shrugged. "Why would you say that?"

"Because," Leo said, staring back at Evan, his expression hard, "ever since we started dating, it's seemed like this relationship has been you, me, and Clay. Every time I turn around, you're going somewhere with Clay, or he's coming over here."

"Clay's my best friend. We've known each other since we were roommates in high school. He's like family." Evan shook his head. "So you're saying I couldn't have friends!" Evan found himself yelling, and he took a deep breath. That wasn't going to get either of them anywhere. "I'm sorry you felt that way. I honestly didn't know." Evan began drawing back. There was no use arguing with Leo because it wasn't going to change anything. "I loved you, Leo," Evan said softly, "I really did." Evan felt his legs start shaking, and he sat back on the sofa. The hurt and pain were already welling inside as he tried not to embarrass himself by breaking into tears. He could do that when he was alone.

"I'm sorry, Evan, I really am," Leo said as he knelt in front of him. "I wish it would have worked out too." Evan felt Leo's hand touch his for just a second, the heat they'd always shared surging through him until Leo's fingers slipped away, and Evan watched as he stood back up. Leo didn't turn around. A few seconds later, he heard the door open and close. Gasping for air, Evan reached for a tissue and let his body tumble onto the sofa as the tears came. He didn't try to stop them as he mourned yet another person who'd left him.

"Damn it," Evan yelled out loud as he punched one of the sofa cushions. He'd really thought Leo could be someone he could be with forever. He'd been kind, thoughtful, and he always seemed to make Evan feel like the most important person in the world. But maybe Evan hadn't made Leo feel the same way. Sitting up slowly, Evan wiped his eyes and sniffed a few times before getting to his feet. There was no use doing all this mushy crap, anyway.

Walking to the kitchen, Evan saw the remains of the breakfast he'd been making for Leo, the bacon now cold on the paper towels and the French toast mixture sitting in the bowl. Not knowing what else to do, Evan turned on the stove. While the pan heated, Evan put away the second set of dishes and then finished making breakfast.

Sitting at the table, Evan stared at the food uneaten before pushing the plate away. A knock at his door gave him a real excuse to give up on it, not that he was hungry in the least now. Carrying his mug of coffee with him so he'd have something to do with his hands, Evan opened the door. "Evan," his neighbor squealed excitedly, "do you have any milk? I was making your French toast recipe and…." Wendy's excitement faded away as she saw the table. "I'm sorry, I interrupted," she added, looking around the room. "Is Leo here?" she asked, and Evan shook his head, moving back into the apartment with Wendy following, closing the door behind her. "Are you okay?"

"No," Evan answered sitting on the sofa, nearly spilling his coffee as he did.

"What happened?" Wendy asked as she sat next to him, and Evan noticed she was still in her bathrobe and slippers, not that it mattered to him in the least.

"Leo," was all Evan managed to say before the tears took over. Wendy hugged him tightly and held him as he let go of some of the confused pain.

"I know, Evan, I know," Wendy crooned softly in his ear. She did know. Wendy was always falling in love and seemed to be one of those people destined to have her heart broken again and again. Evan had held her through a number of breakups, but he never expected she'd be doing it for him. "Men are complete pigs," Wendy said softly, parroting back what Evan always told her, and for a second it made him smile. "How about this?" she asked. "Let me go get dressed and I'll come back this afternoon with ice cream and enough crap to send us into a sugar coma, and we'll watch old movies and stuff until our brains leak out our ears." Wendy could conjure up an image faster than anyone Evan had ever met, and like now, it usually made him smile.

"Thanks, Wendy," Evan muttered, as he wiped his eyes on a tissue. "I'd appreciate the company."

"No sweat," she said with a smile, squeezing one of Evan's knees before getting to her feet. "You've done this for me enough times." Evan turned and watched her leave the apartment.

Sitting on the sofa and staring at the walls as his coffee went cold didn't seem to be helping things, so eventually Evan got himself onto his feet, cleaning up the remains of his uneaten breakfast. He tidied up the kitchen before wandering through the apartment. Pulling out some papers, he tried working, but it didn't work—he was way too distracted and gave up, turning on the television while waiting for Wendy to return for their man-bashing afternoon.

A loud knock on the door made Evan jump. Turning down the television, he got up and answered it. Clay hurried into the apartment. "Don't you answer your phone? I've called three times."

"It never rang." Evan walked to the table, picking up the now-dead phone. "I must have forgotten to charge it." Evan walked into the kitchen and found the cord in the drawer, plugging in the phone. "What's so important?" Evan asked when he returned.

Clay had taken off his coat, throwing it over the back of the sofa. "You look like hell."

"Thank you very much."

"No," Clay said, his voice softening, "I mean something's happened. What's wrong?" Evan remembered that tone of voice. It rang in his ears as his mind flashed back to the day Evan had told Clay about Brother Renier. Clay had used that same almost loving tone then as well.

"Leo broke up with me this morning, so I apologize if I'm not my usual sparkly self," Evan snarked. "Sorry," he said almost immediately, "it's not your fault. I'm just feeling a little bruised."

Evan found himself enclosed in a warm hug, arms holding him tightly. "I'm sorry. I know he meant a lot to you," Clay said softly, comforting him the way he had years before, and for a few seconds, it felt like they were back there. "It'll be okay, you know that," Clay told him, and Evan felt a hand gently stroking his hair as Clay inhaled deeply. For a second, Evan let himself imagine Clay was inhaling his scent, because he was sure as hell getting a nose full of Clay's. Light cologne, slight musk with a hint of soapy cleanliness, had his mind reeling. He'd missed this so much. Closing his eyes, he felt transported back to their small room with its two beds, a room that would forever in his mind carry Clay's scent. Evan took the comfort Clay offered, enjoying being close to his friend. Almost instantly, the old longing and wishes came roaring to the front again.

Slowly backing away, he gazed into Clay's eyes and for just a second caught a glimpse of the look Clay had given him that last night at school years before. That was the one and only time anyone had ever looked at him with such single-minded passion. That look was indelibly etched into his brain. Not sure he was seeing things correctly, Evan blinked, and the look was gone. Stepping back, Evan took a deep breath, looking away from Clay to anywhere else in the room. Leo had just broken up with him, and he was already jonesing on Clay. He shouldn't be feeling like this. Clay was his best friend and was still engaged to be married. Granted, it was to that frigid bitch, Sheila, the Ice Queen herself. What Clay saw in her, Evan would never know, but nonetheless he was still engaged. "Sorry, Clay," Evan mumbled, "I'm a little messed up right now." Grabbing a tissue from the box, Evan blew his nose and took a deep steadying breath. "Somehow I doubt you rushed over because of me and Leo. What's up?"

"I got a call from child services, forwarded from my office, this morning. They have a child for you. He's just turned four, and his parents died in a car accident a few weeks ago. They're willing to place him with you, and you can decide if you want to adopt him. The thing is, they'd like to place him in a proper home as soon as possible. They're willing to bring him by this afternoon."

Evan felt his heart pound in his chest. "Today? They want to place him here today?" Evan wasn't sure he could do it; the emotional whiplash seemed a little overwhelming.

"Yes. And you're absolutely perfect for this child. You know what he's going through, and you'll give him the love and care he needs. I know you will."

Evan wiped his eyes, thinking of that little boy going through at four what he'd gone through at fifteen. He hadn't handled it well at all, and he could only imagine how a youngster like that would deal with losing both parents. "Doesn't he have any other family?" Evan found himself reaching for another tissue.

"Yes, but they're either unwilling or unable to care for him." Clay pulled his phone out of his coat. "What do you want me to tell them?"

"That we'll be right down to meet him," Evan answered, his emotions all over the map, but screw it, screw Leo, and everyone else. This was what he'd wanted and what he'd worked for. Just because Leo had dumped him was no reason not to give a child a home.

"Oh God, Wendy," Evan said, and opened the door, seeing her standing outside about to knock, a bag in her arms.

"What's going on?" Wendy asked as she stepped inside looking from Evan to Clay. "Did something else happen?"

"You could say that. When it rains it pours. Clay told me there's a boy who needs a home and…."

Wendy grinned, setting down the bag on the coffee table. "Sounds like you've got something better to do than pig out and watch movies."

"I'm sorry, but…."

Instead of being mad as Evan thought she might be, Wendy pulled him into a hug. "Leo was a complete ass to let you go. If you were straight, I'd have my hooks in you so deep, you'd never get free." Releasing the hug, Wendy picked up the bag again. "I mean it, Evan. You're one of the best men I've ever met." Wendy grinned once again. "Go get your son."

"They'll only place him with me temporarily," Evan clarified.

Wendy appeared to have none of it, shaking her head as she walked toward the door. Opening it, she gave him another grin. "I don't believe that for a second," she said before closing the door behind her.

Turning away, Evan saw Clay closing his phone. "They'll be ready for us in two hours, and we've got work to do."

"Work?" Evan asked wondering what Clay was talking about.

"One of the conditions is that Nicolas has his own room. You've been planning for that, but you need to get the desk out of there and the bed and dresser you have in the corner set up as well. It would also help for the room to look like a little boy's room."

"I know, but up to now, I didn't know if I would be getting a boy or a girl."

"Now you know." Clay strode toward the door. "I'll be back in a few minutes. Get your desk out of the room, and I'll help you set up the rest." The words had barely reached his ears and Clay was gone in a burst of energy.

Head spinning, Evan tried not to think about Leo or the fact he was going to be a dad, or anything else, for that matter. It was all too much. Maybe this wasn't such a good thing after all.

Walking to the second bedroom, Evan pulled out the desk—thankfully it was on wheels—and unplugged the lamp and laptop. Wheeling it across the hall, he pushed it into the far corner. It was a little cramped, but it would do for now. Plugging everything in again, he looked around his room and repositioned the bed slightly to make a larger path around the desk. That done, he found himself hurrying back.

His own excited energy began to take over, brushing aside his doubts. Positioning the small white dresser against the wall beneath the small window, Evan got to work putting the matching twin bed together. The apartment door opened and banged closed just as he got the bed frame together. Clay waddled in the door, carrying what must have been a box of backbreaking proportions. "What's all this?" Evan asked, helping Clay set the box down.

"When I couldn't get you on the phone, I was already on my way, so I stopped at Target. I knew you didn't have much in here, so I got some things." Clay began pulling purchases out of the box. "I hope Nicolas likes boats," Clay said as he pulled a lamp out of the box in the shape of a sailboat with the mast as the lamp, a white keel, and bright red and blue sails. "I also got a set of sheets." He handed them to Evan, who stared in disbelief, unable to believe Clay's thoughtfulness.

"You didn't have to do this," Evan said as Clay pulled out a sailboat rug that matched the lamp, spreading it on the wood floors.

"It's just a few things to make the room feel cheerier," Clay answered, but Evan knew it was more than that. Clay was taking care of him again, just like he had when they were in school. "Finish getting the bed together and made up," Clay commanded with a huge grin before placing a comforter covered with cartoon boats near the footboard.

"What else is in there?" Evan asked, thinking the box was starting to behave like Mary Poppins's bag, and that a floor lamp and God knew what else were about to make an appearance.

"That's it," Clay pronounced, and he helped Evan make up the bed before checking out the room. "It's a little sparse, but it'll do for now. He may have some things of his own too."

"Thank you, Clay," Evan said, swallowing and taking a deep breath. Damn, he was emotional today. He knew why, but that wasn't helping. "We should go," Evan said, covering his raw emotions with activity. "How did you know I was going to say yes?" Damn, it took a lot of effort to keep his voice from breaking.

"I didn't know about this business with Leo, and for the record, I want to kill the loser for hurting you, but I know you, remember? I knew you'd never be able to say no to a child going through what you went through." Clay broke the box down. "Let's go get your son," Clay said forcefully before leaving the room.

"Clay," Evan called as he followed, "he's… hell, I don't even know Nicolas. What if he doesn't like me? What if they decide to give him to someone else?" Evan caught up with Clay in the living room.

"I already checked it out. I'm a lawyer, remember? Nicolas has no parents or relatives who can take him. He needs a good home, and you can and are willing to provide one, so unless you decide you don't want him, that's not going to happen." Clay stopped and Evan watched him step way too close for normal conversation. "And as for the rest, that little boy will love you the same as I love you." Clay walked toward the door, and Evan stopped dead still, staring at Clay, wondering if he realized what he'd said.

Evan grabbed a jacket, turning out the lights before following Clay out into the hall. Locking the door, they walked toward the elevator, Evan still mulling Clay's inadvertent declaration through his mind.

"My car's over here," Evan said when they reached the sidewalk.

"I know," Clay responded, walking in the other direction, "and mine's over here, and I have the child seat." Clay gave him a sly grin, and Evan joined him walking toward the car.

Traffic was a bear through downtown, and they seemed to catch each and every traffic light. "So have you and Sheila set a date for the wedding?" Clay shook his head, inching the car through the intersection before stopping at the backup for the next light. "Is there a problem?"

At first Evan thought Clay wasn't going to answer, but then he turned toward him, looking anguished. "I don't know. Since I proposed, we really haven't talked about it. She's still wearing the ring, but something isn't right. She graduated from law school last winter and has a job out East, and I have my job here." Clay scratched an itch on his head, adding to his air of confusion. "I thought she was going to get a job here in town so we could be together, but that didn't happen."

"You need to talk to her," Evan said softly, secretly more than happy things weren't going well with the Ice Queen, while at the same time sad for Clay that he was going through this. His own feelings for Clay aside, he wanted him to be happy.

"I know," Clay sighed, "I've just been so busy." Evan had so much he wanted to say. Hell, he wanted to reach over and shake him until he saw things straight, or better yet, kiss him until he was seeing straight, or gay, in this case. Keeping quiet instead, he looked up as they pulled into the office of child services.

Walking through the building toward the caseworker's office, Evan felt as though a million butterflies had lodged in his stomach. "I'm so nervous."

"Don't be. You've already been through the hard part." Clay tried to be encouraging, but it fell flat.

Evan stopped, staring at Clay as though he were stupid. "That was just paperwork and bureaucracy," Evan groused. He was a schoolteacher—he'd been through worse. "This is the hard part, meeting someone who could be part of your life forever."

"Sorry," Clay responded understandingly. "Sometimes I get too caught up in the legal crap. It's a hazard of the job. And you're right." Clay stopped them outside an office. "Take a deep breath and relax. Margaret is here to do her best for Nicolas," Clay explained to Evan, looking him in the eye. "And the best thing for that little boy is you. Never doubt that, because I sure don't."

"How can you not?" Evan asked in a whisper.

"Because you're the best person I've ever known." Clay held his gaze for a few seconds, and Evan wanted to see that same look every day for the rest of his life. "I mean it."

Evan nodded, slowly releasing the breath he'd been holding, and Clay turned the knob, opening the door to the office.

"Mr. Donaldson?" asked a middle-aged woman standing near a desk as he walked in. "I'm Margaret Henderson," she said with a slight smile. "I believe we met briefly during one of your interviews."

"Yes." Evan stepped forward. "It's nice to meet you again." He shook her hand and sat in the chair she indicated while Clay sat in the other. She perched herself on the edge of the desk. "Nicolas came to us a few weeks ago after his parents were killed in an accident," Margaret explained, her voice level and businesslike. "We tried to place him with relatives, but none were suitable, to say the least."

"Clay told me all this earlier," Evan said as he nodded his understanding.

"It's important that you understand this is a traumatized little boy. He's been staying in temporary foster care, and he hasn't been very responsive, not that we can blame him. I just want you to know what to expect." She looked at him appraisingly and said, "In the interview I sat in on, you told us about the death of your parents and that stuck with me."

"Can I see him?" Evan asked nervously, his stomach quaking.

"Of course." Margaret straightened herself up. "He's down the hall in our daycare center."

Evan stood up, following Margaret out of the office and through the hallway of the office building, noticing quite a few lights on. "Do a lot of people work Saturdays?" Evan asked, curious.

"It's one of the things you learn really quickly in this line of work." Margaret stopped walking, turning toward him as she said, "Children need help no matter what day it is."

"I understand, believe me," Evan said before adding, "and you have to help them one at a time. Sometimes in the classroom, you can teach the entire class, but the biggest leaps in understanding happen at different times for each student. I suspect it's the same for you. We create programs to help, but when push comes to shove, each child's needs are different." Evan hoped to hell he wasn't coming off like an idiot. He was so nervous, he felt like he was rambling.

Margaret smiled before starting to walk again. "There's nothing to be nervous about," she said, turning to smile at Clay knowingly. Evan wondered what that was about, but before he could ask, they stopped at a doorway, and Evan peered inside. "Nicolas is the blond sitting alone at the table near the wall."

"He looks like he's coloring," Evan breathed softly, like his voice would carry into the room and he'd disturb him. Evan felt a chill run up his spine, and he turned to Clay, looking for reassurance.

His best friend smiled back at him, nodding slowly. "Go on in and say hello."

Pushing the door open, Evan stepped into the room, and the children looked up at him, breaking their play, all of them except Nicolas, who remained engrossed in what he was doing. Margaret walked to a table where one of the adults watched over the scene. Evan barely noticed, his complete attention focused on Nicolas. Walking slowly toward the table, Evan sat in one of the child-sized chairs, watching Nicolas as he colored. "I'm Evan. What's your name?"

"Nicolas," the little boy answered, barely looking up from his task.

"What are you drawing?" Evan asked quietly. Nicolas looked up, big blue eyes going straight to Evan's heart. Glancing back toward Clay, Evan steadied his nerves before pointing to one of the figures on the paper. "Who's that?"

"Momma," Nicolas answered before returning to his drawing. "That's Daddy." Evan felt the tears well in his eyes, and he turned away for a second, wiping them away. "They're in heaven now. I'm staying in a home until they come back for me."

"Nicolas," Evan started quietly, his voice nearly breaking, "your mom and dad died, and they aren't coming back."

The little boy lifted his eyes from the drawing. "I know. I just like to pretend sometimes." Nicolas put his crayon down, blue eyes glistening with tears. "I miss them." His lower lip began to quiver. Reacting on instinct, Evan pulled the little boy into a hug, letting him cry on his shoulder.

"I know you do, and it's okay to miss them. They miss you too. They can't be with you right now, but they're looking down on you from heaven."

"Like angels?" Nicolas asked with a sniff.

"Exactly, just like angels." Evan found himself sniffling as he answered. Peering over Nicolas's shoulder, he saw Clay walk to him, handing him a tissue before settling a hand on his shoulder. Evan let Nicolas cry it out, giving him all the time he wanted. "Do you see the lady over there?"

Nicolas looked to where Evan pointed. "Miss Margaret?"

"Yes. She called me today and asked if I could give you a home. Is that okay? Would you like to come home with me to live?" Evan knew whatever happened, this had to be Nicolas's choice. "I have a room all set up for you," Evan said before continuing. "Do you like sailboats?" Nicolas nodded. "It has a sailboat lamp and a boat bedspread. Would you like to come see it?"

Nicolas nodded slowly, and Evan lifted him into his arms, standing up as he walked back toward where Margaret waited. He felt Nicolas squirm, and turning around, he saw Clay picking up the drawing before handing it to Nicolas. "Who's that?" Nicolas asked after taking his drawing.

"That's my friend Clay."

With Nicolas holding his drawing, Evan carried him out of the daycare center and back toward Margaret's office. "I have a few things you need to sign and a few questions." Evan nodded, holding Nicolas tightly, even as the little boy held on to him. Sitting in a chair in Margaret's office, signing the papers was difficult, but Evan refused to let go of Nicolas, and Nicolas seemed just as determined to hold on to Evan.

"Do you have daycare for Nicolas while you're at work?" Margaret asked, her pen hovering over Nicolas's file.

"Yes. They offer daycare at the school." He was sure he'd supplied that information before.

"I'll stop by later in the week to see how you're getting on, and we can arrange for a grief counselor for Nicolas once he's settled," Margaret said as she slid the signed papers into a file.

"Come Thursday for dinner if you like," Evan said, and Margaret smiled. "I don't know what we'll be having, but you're welcome." Standing up, he thanked her. He would have shaken her hand, but he had his arms full. She seemed to understand. "Where are his things?" Evan asked.

"His parents didn't leave much, but I've got his suitcase here. There are a few other things, which I'll bring when I stop by." Clay lifted the suitcase, and they headed toward the door. "Mr. Donaldson," she called, "thank you."

Evan nodded a little. "Nicolas, say goodbye to Miss Margaret." Evan used the term Nicolas had used on purpose, and watched as he waved to her, rubbing his eyes as they left the office. "Clay has your suitcase and drawing. Are you hungry?" Nicolas nodded his head, but didn't speak. "Where do you want to go? We can go anywhere you like."

"Home. I wanna go home to Momma." Nicolas rested his head on Evan's shoulder and began to cry again. Evan rubbed his back, soothing as best he could.

"I know," was all he could say. He did know exactly how he felt. "Do you want to stop at McDonald's?" Evan asked softly, and Nicolas nodded against his shoulder. "Okay." They walked out of the building to Clay's car. Evan strapped Nicolas into his seat, sitting in the back next to Nicolas as Clay pulled out of the parking lot and out into traffic. It took a while with traffic, but Clay pulled into a McDonald's a little before noon. The place was crowded, and Evan held Nicolas's hand as they walked across the parking lot.

Inside, it was noisy and loud. Nicolas turned toward him, hands over his ears, face buried in one of Evan's legs. Reaching down, Evan lifted Nicolas, holding him. "It's just noise. It's okay," he soothed. Nicolas lowered his hands and rested his head on Evan's shoulder. He could so get used to that.

"See, I told you you'd make a great dad," Clay said softly from beside him.

"What would you like? A Happy Meal?" Evan asked, and Nicolas nodded. "With a hamburger or chicken nuggets?"

"Nuggets," Nicolas said softly into his ear, holding Evan tightly around the neck.

"Clay, would you place the order? I'm going to try to find a quieter place."

"Of course." Clay smiled, and Evan walked through the restaurant, around the corner toward the back, and the noise level dropped significantly.

"Better?" Evan asked, setting Nicolas on the seat. "What do you like to do besides draw pretty pictures?" Nicolas shrugged his shoulders. "Do you like to go to the playground?"

"Yes. I like to swing," Nicolas answered quietly.

"Would you like to go to the park tomorrow? We can swing, and you can go down the slide." Evan talked with enthusiasm, but Nicolas wasn't buying it. He simply nodded and looked back at him. The lost look in the little boy's eyes was enough to wrench Evan's heart from his chest. Clay set the tray on the table, and Evan set Nicolas's food in front of him. Nicolas knelt on the seat and ate a few French fries, scanning the room over and over again.

Evan tried his best to eat, but found himself watching every move Nicolas made, and nearly jumped when he felt Clay's hand touch his. "He's okay, Evan. Things are just new for him, and he needs to process things." Evan wasn't sure he was buying that, but forced himself to relax a little. Looking at the tray in front of him, he saw that Clay had gotten him a salad with low-fat dressing and a Diet Coke. Clay winked. "Did you think I didn't know what you wanted? Go ahead and eat."

Evan worked on his salad, keeping an eye on Nicolas, who ate about half his food. "Nicky, do you want to go play in there?" Clay asked, pointing to the play area with tubes and play balls. Clay got up, setting aside his food, and reached for Nicolas, who went with him. Evan continued eating as he saw Clay help Nicolas take off his shoes. He didn't run around like the other kids, and Evan found himself rushing through his lunch.

Through the window he saw Clay pointing out things, and Nicolas looked back at him. Clay walked Nicolas around to one of the ladders, holding his hand as he climbed. At the top, Nicolas looked back, and Clay nodded, obviously encouraging him. Evan saw Nicolas disappear from sight, popping up again at the bottom of the slide. And he smiled. Evan knew he'd always remember that moment for as long as he lived. He saw Clay lift Nicolas off his feet, both of them smiling, and he wished he had a camera. Fishing in his pocket, Evan pulled out his phone. Leaving the table, he walked to the door, clicking it open. He could hear Clay's voice say, "You can do it, Nicky."

Nicolas, more confident now, scampered up the ladder before sliding down again. He didn't laugh or scream like the other kids, but at the bottom he smiled again, and Evan snapped a picture with his phone. He snapped another when Clay scooped Nicolas out of the balls, holding him. For a second, both of them smiled, unaware he was watching, and Evan snapped another picture. He had no idea how good they were, but it didn't matter. "Are you both finished eating?"

Nicolas ignored the question, and Clay nodded. After returning to the table and dumping the trash, he returned to the play area. "Evan, you play too," Nicolas said, taking his hand and pulling him toward the balls.

"Yeah, Ev, you play too," Clay teased.

Eventually they both stood near one of the windows, watching Nicolas play. Evan could feel Clay near him, close and comforting. "Thank you," Evan said softly, not taking his eyes off Nicolas.

"Ev," Clay said softly, almost pleading, and Evan turned toward him, watching as Clay swallowed, but he didn't say anything more. Evan felt an old, familiar longing, one that had become part of his daily life at school and for years afterward. During the months he was with Leo, it had abated a great deal, but it was back once again like an old muscle injury on a cold morning, letting you know it was still there.

Nicolas came to him, and Evan pulled himself out of his longings. "Are you ready to see your new room?" Evan asked, and Nicolas nodded, looking around him once again before letting Evan help him with his shoes.

By the time they'd parked near Evan's building, Nicolas had nearly fallen asleep in his car seat. But as soon as they stopped, his eyes slid open. "I'll get the suitcase and meet you inside," Clay told him from the front seat, and Evan nervously helped Nicolas out of the car seat. Holding hands, they walked into the building with Clay following behind.

Nicolas hated the elevator, holding on to Evan the entire time they were moving. When it stopped and the doors parted, he ran out, waiting in the hallway for them. "That's where we live," Evan said pointing toward his door. Nicolas simply looked at him, and Evan took Nicolas's hand, watching as the boy turned to see if Clay was coming too. Evan unlocked the door, and Nicolas took a step inside, stopping and refusing to go any farther. "What is it?" Evan asked, turning on the lights. "There's nothing to be afraid of." Evan took Nicolas's hand, leading him around the apartment, showing him everything. At the bathroom, Nicolas indicated he had to go. "Do you need help?"

Nicolas shook his head, and Evan stood outside the door, fretting until he heard the toilet flush and the lid clunk down again.

"What's in there?" Nicolas asked softly after joining Evan in the hallway, staring at the closed bedroom door.

"That's your room," Evan said, looking to Clay as he opened the door. Nicolas walked inside, looking around before running to the bed, jumping onto the mattress. "Do you like it?"

"I like boats," Nicolas said as he squirmed on the bed. Clay came in after them, bringing the suitcase and laying it on the bed near Nicolas, who clumsily popped open the latches, pulling out an old, once-white stuffed bunny with big floppy ears. Hugging it close, Nicolas curled on the bed, his head resting on the pillow, yawning, ignoring everything else. Evan wasn't sure what he should do and found himself walking to the bed, giving Nicolas a hug. Setting the suitcase on the floor near the foot of the bed, Evan slid a blanket over his half sleeping child before leaving the room with Clay. Leaving the door partly ajar, Evan walked slowly toward the living room, almost afraid to breathe.

"He's going to be fine, Evan," Clay reassured him as he sat on the sofa. "He seems completely taken with you."

"You too. He actually smiled." Evan pulled out his phone, showing Clay the pictures.

"I know, but did you see the way he keeps looking around all the time?"

"Yeah, I think he's looking for his mom and dad. He doesn't understand that they're gone and not coming back," Evan said, wondering what he should do. "I know he will in time, but it's heartbreaking."

Clay agreed. "But you're just the person to help him and love him. Heck, Evan, you already do. That little boy has your heart already."

"Not all of it," Evan replied softly, unsure of what he wanted to say.

"I know today has been a bit of a whirlwind for you, with the crap with Leo this morning and now this, but would you change anything?"

Evan nodded his head. "Yeah, I would," he answered, but he didn't elaborate. Getting up from the sofa, Evan began walking toward the kitchen but couldn't remember what it was he wanted when he got there. Walking back into the living room, he found Clay staring up at him expectantly from the sofa. "What happened to you, Clay?"

"What do you mean?"

Evan stepped closer, keeping his voice low. "Clay, you know very well what I'm referring to. That last night at St. Bart's. What happened?"

Clay squirmed on the sofa. "I grew up, Evan. We were kids."

"You grew up," Evan said levelly, crossing his arms in front of his chest. "So I was just some childish whim, is that it?"

"No," Clay answered very quickly. "You were never a whim, but I needed to grow up."

"So you said," Evan responded as he glared at his best friend. "That night at St. Bart's was the most memorable night of my life. I finally got to make love with the one person who meant more to me than anyone else in the world, and I thought it meant something to you too. But I guess I was wrong."

"You really loved me?" Clay asked, surprise showing in his eyes.

"Of course I did. I've loved you for years, but now I think it was just me holding on to a stupid childish notion I should have let go of a long time ago. Hell, no wonder things didn't work out with Leo."

"What's he got to do with this?" Clay countered defensively.

"When I saw him this morning, he said he always felt as though our relationship had three people in it—him, me, and you. And he was right, because I never let you go, not fully. But I think it's something I have to do now. I've been carrying a torch for you since high school, and I think it's time I let it go out."

Clay seemed surprised and maybe a little shocked. "Evan, you're my best friend, the best friend I've ever had. I don't want to lose you."

"We can be friends, Clay, but I think I need some space right now. I know you don't feel the same way about me that I feel for you. You just have to give me a little space to work things out, and you need to decide what you want. I doubt the Ice Queen is really the companion you want for the rest of your life, otherwise you'd have moved on with your relationship, but I'm not what you want, either, and I need to accept that." Clay stood up and moved closer, but Evan backed away. "This isn't your fault, Clay, I know that. You just need to give me a little time." Evan felt the bubble of denial around his emotions burst. "You know, I always thought I could live with you just being my friend, but I don't think I can do that anymore."

"But, Ev, it's not that simple." Clay looked torn and a little lost.

Evan stepped forward, leaning toward Clay as he pressed their lips together. Holding Clay tightly, he kissed him with everything he had, throwing years of repressed love, care, even hurt, into that one single kiss. Gentling it, he backed away again. "There. If the Ice Queen can equal that, you're perfect for each other."

A rustling from the far end of the hall caught his attention, and Evan moved toward Nicolas's room. "You need to decide what you want, Clay." Turning his back, he walked to Nicolas's room, pushing the door open, peering inside. Nicolas tossed on the bed, rolling first one way and then the other. Walking into the room,

Evan sat on the edge of the bed, rubbing the boy's back until he stopped moving and settled back to sleep. Sitting with Nicky, Evan heard the apartment door close. Clay was gone… again… and Evan half wanted to run and get him back.

"Daddy?" Nicolas questioned as he slid his eyes open, looking up at Evan, his eyes huge.

"It's Evan, remember? You're here with me now, and it's okay. Everything's going to be okay." While the words were meant for Nicolas, he wondered if he wasn't trying to soothe himself as well. Lifting Nicolas out of the bed, Evan carried him into the living room as Nicolas, still clutching his bunny, rested his head on Evan's shoulder.

"I want Momma," Nicolas whimpered softly, still holding on to Evan.

"I know you do," Evan answered softly, sitting down on the sofa. "When I wasn't much older than you," Evan explained, exaggerating a little, but knowing he needed to help, "my mama and papa died too."

Nicolas lifted his head, looking into Evan's eyes. "Did you end up in a 'fosser' home too?"

"I did," Evan admitted. "But you're not in a foster home anymore. You can stay here with me for as long as you like."

"Until Momma and Daddy come back?" Nicolas asked, rubbing the sleep out of his eyes.

Evan shook his head slowly. He knew he had to be honest. It was the only way. "Your mama and daddy aren't coming back. They're in heaven, remember? But I'm going to love you and take care of you just like they would if they were here. I promise. I won't let anything happen to you. Okay?" Evan nodded his head slowly.

"Okay," Nicolas said, squirming to get down onto the floor.

"Would you like some juice?"

"Yes," Nicolas said.

"Yes, what?"

"Yes, please," Nicolas answered, and Evan got up from the sofa, extending his hand, leading Nicolas to the kitchen. Evan opened the cabinet, digging around for a paper cup before finding some apple juice. "Looks like we need to go to the store. Sh—" Evan cut himself off before the naughty word passed his lips. He needed so much for Nicolas. "Let's see if there's something on television."

Nicolas raced into the living room, sitting cross-legged on the rug in the middle of the floor. Evan found a station, and Nicolas almost immediately engrossed himself in *Sesame Street*. Evan collapsed onto the sofa, his mind spinning over everything that had happened. Leo had dumped him, and for all intents and purposes, Evan had sent Clay away. God, he felt like he'd made a mess of everything. Clay had helped him with all the legalities and paperwork. Heck, he'd even brought over all that stuff for Nicolas's room. Hanging his head, Evan wondered how he could have acted like such an ass to him. Reaching over, Evan almost picked up his phone to apologize. What could he say? Damn it, he should have just kept his mouth shut.

Evan heard a soft knock on the door. Getting up to answer it, he found Wendy smiling back at him. "Come in. I have someone I'd like you to meet." Evan smiled, motioning her inside. "Wendy, this is Nicolas." Nicolas looked up from the television, looking warily at their visitor. "Nicolas, this is Wendy. She's our neighbor. Come say hello."

Getting up, he walked over, hiding behind Evan's legs, saying nothing. Wendy knelt down. "Hello, I'm Wendy."

"It's okay, Nicolas. She's really nice," Evan prodded lightly, but he refused to come out, so Evan picked him up, holding him while Nicolas buried his face in Evan's shoulder.

Wendy stood back up. "It looks like you've had quite a day."

Evan sighed. "You don't know the half of it."

"Do we need the ice cream?" Wendy could always be counted on for comfort food. "I'll be right back with the cookies 'n cream." She was gone before Evan could say boo, returning a few minutes later with a half gallon of ice cream that had Nicolas smiling.

"Stay here," Evan told him, "and I'll bring you a bowl."

Evan met Wendy in the kitchen. "He's adorable," she said, scooping two bowls and a smaller one for Nicolas.

"But still traumatized by his parents' death. It'll get easier, but he'll need some time," Evan said as he got a dishcloth and spoons. Wendy put the ice cream container in the freezer, and they carried the bowls into the living room. Placing the towel over Nicolas's lap, he gave him the bowl and joined Wendy on the sofa.

"Okay, spill it," Wendy said, curling her feet beneath her.

"You know about Leo and getting Nicky," Evan began before telling her all about Clay. He told her everything about how he'd first fallen for him in high school, their night together, Clay's engagement, their friendship, how he still felt about him, everything. By the time he was done, his ice cream was gone, and he was definitely thinking about a refill. "I don't know what to do."

Wendy sat her bowl aside. "If you ask me, I think he probably has feelings for you, too, but he isn't ready to face them. You said he kept saying he grew up. Are those his thoughts or the Ice Queen's?"

"You think?" Evan asked suddenly hopeful again.

"Don't know, I'm just asking," she answered as Nicolas got up from the floor, bringing Evan his empty bowl and the towel before returning to his place in front of the television. "Do you really love him?"

"I always have. That's the problem, I guess. I thought friendship was enough, but it's not. I want more. But I guess I'm realizing that maybe I don't need anyone." Evan let his gaze drift to Nicolas, lying on his stomach, chin on his hands, engrossed in the TV program. "Maybe I have to be strong for myself and him."

Wendy chuckled, shaking her head. "You've always been strong, but you just never let yourself feel it. You had the strength to let Leo go because you wanted more, and look, you got Nicolas. Your time will come, but I think you were right about Clay. I know it sounds cliché, but you had to let him go. If it's meant to be, you'll be together."

Evan stopped, suddenly startled as a thought long-forgotten came back to him. "That's what Father Val said the last time I spoke to him. Maybe he was right, and we weren't meant for each other."

"Or maybe the time isn't right yet. Either way, you have Nicolas to take care of." Wendy stood up, picking up the bowls to take to the kitchen. "Just concentrate on being a dad for a while and let the rest take care of itself." Looking at Nicolas, Evan thought that was probably the best piece of advice he'd been given in a long time. If only it were that easy.

Chapter 6

EVAN woke as he had for the past month, listening for any sound from Nicolas's room. Hearing none, he settled back into the darkness, thinking. He hadn't heard a word from Clay the entire time, and it worried him. Evan had spent the last month beating himself up over what he'd said and the way he'd acted toward his best friend, probably ex-best friend now. He'd talked to both Dex and Frankie, but neither of them had heard from Clay either. He'd told them both about the disagreement, but even when pressed, had refused to tell them what it was about. To tell the truth, Evan was embarrassed and ashamed of his behavior. He should have talked to Clay rather than turning their conversation into an inquisition, or at least that's how he was remembering it. He missed his friend terribly.

He hadn't wasted his first month with Nicolas. Usually during the summer he got a seasonal job to earn extra money and keep himself busy, but this year he'd foregone that, so he and Nicolas had spent a lot of time together. Nicky, as Evan was now calling him, loved the beach, and they went in the late afternoon two or three days a week. Evan would bring a chair and umbrella so he could sit and read a book while Nicky dug holes and played in the sand around him. He never went far or even touched the water unless Evan took his hand. Evan knew that would end eventually, but he figured he should be grateful while it lasted. All in all, he was happy, but….

An unfamiliar, soft sound reached his ears, and Evan pushed back the covers, pulling on his robe before walking across to Nicky's room. Pushing open the door, he heard him gasping for breath, sounding like he was alternately coughing and choking. "Nicky," he said softly, turning on the sailboat lamp. Scared eyes bored into him as Nicky struggled to breathe. "Relax, I'm here." Evan lifted Nicky out of the bed—he was definitely feverish, his pajamas wet, skin clammy. Grabbing a blanket, he covered him, carrying Nicky to his room. Setting him on his bed, Evan pulled on a pair of pants and the first shirt he could find, slipping on a pair of shoes before lifting Nicky into his arms again. "It's going to be okay," he soothed, trying to keep Nicky calm as his own heart raced a mile a minute.

Hurrying out of the bedroom, he grabbed his wallet and keys before leaving the apartment, calling for the elevator.

"Is everything all right?"

Evan turned. Wendy's head poked out her cracked door. "Nicky's having trouble breathing, and I'm taking him to the hospital."

"Do you want me to go with you?" she asked, but Evan knew she wasn't dressed, and he couldn't wait.

"We'll be fine. I'll call you. I promise." The elevator door opened, and Evan stepped inside. He pressed the ground floor button, and the doors closed. Nicky didn't react the way he usually did, and in the enclosed space, Evan could hear each and every one of Nicky's labored breaths and found himself praying each one wouldn't be his last.

The damned elevator seemed to take forever, and when the doors finally slid open, Evan hurried outside onto the dark street and to his car. Keys still in his hand, he unlocked the doors and set

Nicky in his seat, buckling him in record time. "We're going to get you to a doctor who can help you. Okay?" Evan tried to be soothing, but his nerves were definitely getting the best of him. Starting the car, Evan took off through the nearly empty streets toward the hospital he knew was only a mile or so away.

Pulling into the emergency entrance, he parked the car under the portico and rushed around, unbuckling Nicky and lifting him out of the seat, hurrying toward the doors that parted as he got near. Rushing to the desk, any sense of calm long gone, Evan said hurriedly, "I need some help. He's having trouble breathing."

Nicky clung to him, and his breaths reverberated in Evan's ears, each one increasing his nervousness. "What are his symptoms?" The receptionist asked. Evan shifted Nicky onto his other shoulder, and she heard his labored breathing. "Never mind. Go right on through, and I'll have someone meet you." The door buzzed and Evan carried Nicky through the open door. "Follow me. I've already alerted the doctor," the receptionist said as she passed them, and Evan hurried after her. She led them to a small room, and he placed Nicky on the bed. He looked terrified and would probably be crying aloud if he could have breathed well enough. As it was, tears streaked down his cheeks.

A nurse rushed in. Opening a cabinet, she pulled out a keyboard and began asking all kinds of questions. Evan answered them on autopilot, his attention focused on Nicky. The nurse placed an oxygen mask over Nicky's face, and he immediately tried to pull it away.

"It's okay—that will make you feel better," Evan soothed, rubbing Nicky's arm. She fiddled with things, and Nicky seemed to breathe a little easier once the oxygen began to flow.

After taking his temperature, blood pressure, and pulse, the nurse left, and a few agonizing minutes later a doctor came in. "I'm Doctor Harry," he told them. "What's the problem, little guy?" he asked, focusing his attention on Nicky. "They tell me you're having trouble breathing." The doctor took out his stethoscope, and after helping Nicky sit up, listened to his lungs. Looking to Evan, he asked, "Has he had any coughs or colds lately?"

"No," Evan answered. "Nicky's been healthy and active for the month he's been in my care. I'm his foster father and hope to adopt him, but I know little of his medical history," Evan answered, frustrated that he couldn't be more helpful.

The doctor kept listening. "Is he allergic to anything?"

"Not that I'm aware of. He hasn't eaten anything in the last few days he hasn't eaten before." Evan found some of his nervous energy abating as the doctor looked Nicky over.

"Can you take a big, deep breath for me?" the doctor asked, and Nicky did his best, but struggled, and Evan felt his own breathing stop.

"His lungs are definitely inflamed, but I don't hear fluid, which is very good. I think it may be a virus. We've seen a number of children coming in with breathing problems. Has he been around other kids? At school or a play group?"

"Only the beach."

"That could do it," Doctor Harry said. "We're going to add a little medication to the oxygen. That should bring down the swelling, and we'll give you a nebulizer and medication for him. You'll probably need to use it three times a day to start." The doctor turned his attention to a still-scared Nicky. "You're going to be fine," he said, smiling. "You've been very good and really brave." Nicky peered up at the doctor through the mask. "I need to talk to your daddy a minute. Will you be okay with the nurse? We'll be just out there, I promise."

The nurse came back in, and Evan stepped out with the doctor, staying where Nicky could see him. "I'd like to keep him here for the next few hours just to be sure everything's okay," the doctor told him. "As I said, I think it's a virus, but I want to rule out asthma."

"Whatever you need," Evan answered, looking back at Nicky, seeing his big, scared eyes staring back at him.

"I'll be back in a bit to make sure the medication's working."

"Thank you," Evan said and rejoined Nicky, sitting in the chair next to him, holding his small hand in his. Evan pulled out his phone and saw he had a single bar. Without thinking, he pushed a button for speed dial.

"Evan, is that you?"

"Yes, I'm at St. Mary's with Nicky."

"I'll...." Evan stared at the screen as it blinked that the connection had been lost. Nicky began to squirm, and Evan shoved the phone back in his pocket. He thought he'd try calling Wendy back in a few minutes if he could get a signal.

Nicky's huge eyes stared back at him from around the oxygen mask, but at least he appeared to be breathing easier. "Just relax, no one's going to hurt you, I promise," Evan said as he brushed the hair away from Nicky's forehead, finally allowing himself to take a deep breath and hope that everything was going to be all right.

"Mr. Donaldson," a nurse said quietly from the doorway, "there's someone out in the waiting room. They said you called."

"That must be Wendy. I called her a little while ago. Could you send her back?"

The nurse looked surprised. "I don't know who you called, but the man waiting for you is definitely not Wendy. He said his name was Clay."

Clay? He'd called Clay? Pulling out the phone, Evan searched through it, seeing the last number called was indeed Clay's. He must have pressed the wrong speed dial number.

"Could you please send him back?" Evan had no idea what to say to the man.

"Of course," the nurse said softly before disappearing from the doorway. A few minutes later, she returned with Clay right behind her.

"How is he?" Clay asked, hurrying into the room, standing on the other side of Nicky's bed, and looking like he hadn't slept in days.

"He's doing better, and they're giving him some medication right now. They think it's some virus, but they want to rule out asthma, so they'll be taking him for a few tests. I'm sorry I got you out of bed." Evan looked across the bed, his hand still holding Nicky's. "I must have hit the wrong number, and when you answered, I really wasn't listening and…."

"Evan, it's okay," Clay said softly before turning his attention to the wide-eyed little blond boy on the bed. "Are you breathing better?"

Nicky turned his head toward Evan.

"You remember Clay, he helped me bring you home," Evan explained, wishing he could talk to Clay, really talk to him, but now wasn't the time; he knew that.

"Hi, Nicky," the nurse said as she came back in. "We're going to take you for a ride in your bed," she said pleasantly. "They want to take some pictures of your insides. It won't hurt at all, I promise."

Nicky looked to Evan, and he nodded, still holding his hand. "Your daddy will be with you the entire time," the nurse said encouragingly. Evan looked at Nicky, hoping the term wouldn't upset him. They'd never talked about those kinds of terms before. Nicky had called him Evan up to now, and he'd figured Nicky would settle on whatever he was comfortable with. But to Evan's relief, he didn't seem to react other than to watch every move the nurse made, and when she worked behind his head to shift the lines for his mask, he squirmed around, trying to see what she was doing. "I'm just changing the tubes so they can go with you," she explained, making sure everything was placed correctly before unlocking the bed with a metallic thunk, slowly beginning to move the bed out of the room.

"Clay, I...." He figured he needed to say something.

"Don't worry about anything, Ev. I'll be right here when you and Nicky get back," Clay said, moving to sit in the chair as Evan walked away with Nicky.

They traveled through the hallways with Nicky clutching his hand as they moved, eyes clamped shut. "It's okay," Evan kept saying, not sure what he could say to reassure him. They stopped, and the nurse opened the door, wheeling the bed into a darkened room with big machines that made a low humming sound. They placed the bed near the middle of the room.

A woman walked up to the bed, talking to Nicky. "We're just going to take a picture. It won't hurt at all. Is it okay if Daddy puts you on the table?"

Nicky looked at her and then Evan before nodding. Gently picking him up, Evan transferred Nicky to the table while the nurse made sure the tubes were okay. "You're being a brave big boy, Nicky," Evan told him, and he watched as Nicky's eyes followed what everyone was doing. They had Nicky roll onto his side.

"Just hold still, and we'll take the picture and be all done," she said. Evan continued holding Nicky's hand as the machine moved a little and then made a buzzing sound for a second. "Perfect, you're all done."

Evan lifted Nicky back onto the bed, covering him with the blanket. "You were very good," Evan said. "I'm so proud of you."

"Can we go home?" Nicky asked, his voice muffled by the mask. "I don't like this fing," he added, pulling a little at the mask.

"I know, and we'll go home soon. We need to take another ride on the bed to get back to the little room and then wait for the doctor." The brakes released and the bed began to move out of the room and then back down the hall. Nicky didn't seem as upset this time, and when they arrived in the room, he saw Clay and smiled at him.

"Were you a big boy?" Clay asked him, and Nicky smiled and nodded.

"He was super," Evan added, kissing Nicky on the forehead before looking at Clay, wondering what he was thinking and hoping he'd truly have the chance to talk to him. Clay gave him a wan smile, but concentrated his attention on Nicky, whose eyes kept drifting closed before popping open again.

Evan found himself alternately looking at Nicky, then gazing at Clay, before returning to Nicky again. The doctor entering finally, pulled his attention to one spot. "His chest X-ray looks pretty good. There's some inflammation, but it seems to be getting better. I'll give you a prescription for some medication, and we'll send you home with the nebulizer. If you've never used one, the nurse will show you how to use it. I suggest you call his pediatrician in the morning; he'll probably want to see him as well." The doctor moved to Nicky. "I think you're going to be fine, buddy. You were a good boy," he added, handing Nicky a lollipop. "You can have this, but save it until you're feeling better, okay?"

Nicky smiled under the mask, and the doctor left. The nurse returned a short time later, removing the mask, much to Nicky's relief, and showed Evan how to use the nebulizer. After signing some papers, Evan lifted Nicky off the bed and into his arms.

Carrying everything, they made their way to the desk where Evan gave them his insurance card, figuring if that wasn't right, he'd sort it out later. All that mattered now was getting Nicky home. After signing some more papers, they were on their way outside. "Ev, I'll meet you at your place," Clay said, and Evan simply nodded, unlocking the doors before putting Nicky in his seat." The drive home was short, and after getting Nicky out of the car, he met Clay at the door, the man once again carrying everything.

Nicky didn't move when they got in the elevator, he simply held on to Evan, his head on Evan's shoulder. In the apartment, Clay turned on a small lamp in one corner of the living room while Evan sat on the sofa, holding Nicky. "In the second drawer of his dresser are Nicky's pajamas, would you get me a clean set? He's been sweating, and I'd like to change him." Clay nodded and walked to Nicky's room, returning shortly with pajamas and underwear. "Stand up, sweetheart," Evan said softly, and Nicky stood on the sofa, letting Evan strip him down and re-dress him before curling back into Evan's arms.

"Clay, you don't have to stay if you don't want to," Evan whispered, listening to each breath Nicky took. He sounded much better now and even appeared to be falling asleep.

"Ev," Clay said softly, and Evan felt a hand slide along his shoulder. "I'll be fine right here." The fingers felt so warm through his shirt. Evan had to resist the urge to move into the touch. He couldn't let himself read anything more into it than some simple comfort from a friend. "Go on to bed. I'll be fine."

Evan sighed, carefully getting to his feet. "The extra blankets and pillows are in the small closet outside the bathroom."

"I know," Clay said, "I helped you move, remember?"

He did. Clay had carried load after load up from his previous apartment. Leo had said he wasn't feeling well and hadn't been able to help, but Clay had stayed all day, hauling to and from the elevator, even carrying some things up three floors. And Evan had to admit, having Clay here made him feel better. "You always help me with everything," Evan added before walking down the hall.

Pausing outside Nicky's room, he didn't have the heart or the will to put Nicky back in bed, so he carried his son into his room, setting him on the side of the bed nearest the wall. Evan pulled back the covers, and Nicky curled beneath them, his head on the pillow, already nearly asleep. Going into the boy's room, Evan found Nicky's bunny and brought it to him. That was the last thing Nicky seemed to need. Pulling the stuffed animal close, he shut his eyes.

Walking carefully in the dark room, Evan changed into fresh pajamas before getting into the bed. Small noises from the apartment reached his ears, as did the springs creaking on the sofa as Clay moved around. He also heard the soft sounds of Nicky's breathing. For hours, he listened for any sign of trouble, finally falling asleep.

Footsteps in the living room woke him as light filtered in through his small bedroom window. Nicky slept next to him, not having moved all night. His breathing sounded like he had a slight cold, and Evan made a note to himself to get the prescriptions filled as soon as Nicky woke up. Slipping out of the bed, he left the room as quietly as he could, padding through the house until he reached the kitchen, where Clay stood near the refrigerator, half asleep, drinking from an old coffee mug. "Did you sleep?" Clay asked, handing Evan a mug.

"A little, I think. Nicky's still out, which is good. He sounds like he's got a cold. As soon as he gets up, I'll get his prescriptions filled."

Clay drank from his mug before moving into the living room, and Evan followed, joining him on the sofa. "I meant to call you a while ago, but…."

Evan set his mug on the coffee table before stopping him. "It's my fault. I shouldn't have treated you that way. It wasn't right or fair. My feelings for you are my issue, and I shouldn't have made them yours or put conditions on our friendship. That wasn't fair. I can—"

Clay stared back at him. "Ev," Clay said, interrupting, "you were right. Everything you said was right. I was hiding with Sheila, and I broke it off with her a few days ago. I wasn't happy, and I doubt she was either. Evan, you asked me to think about what I wanted, and I have. I've thought about almost nothing else for the last month, and when you called, I couldn't have stayed away if my life had depended on it. I've always been there for you."

"I know you have," Evan muttered. Clay had been a constant support and comfort for him—it was part of the reason he'd fallen for him in the first place.

"Wait, let me finish. I've always been there for you because you've always been there for me. I could always count on your help in school, and afterwards when law school got so overpowering, it was you who convinced me to stick it out and take it one day at a time and one problem at a time. I know we didn't stay in touch as much as we should have, but you were always there, and I knew that." Clay moved closer, and Evan saw him swallow. "Ev, I want—"

"Daddy?"

Evan froze at Nicky's voice. Was he talking to him? It almost seemed too good to be true. Nicky, still rubbing his eyes, walked to the sofa, climbing onto the cushions before settling himself on Evan's lap. "Daddy, I'm hungry. Can I have cimmamon toast?"

Evan thought his heart would burst with joy. Nicky had called him *Daddy*. "You can have anything you want," he answered, relieved that Nicky was okay and elated that he'd been called Daddy for the first time in his life. Evan didn't know what he'd been expecting, but to actually hear the word from Nicky was unexpectedly wonderful. Evan hugged Nicky, looking over his shoulder at Clay, who beamed back at him.

"How about I run to the drugstore to fill Nicky's prescriptions while you feed him," Clay offered. "It shouldn't take very long."

"Don't you have to go to work?"

"It's Sunday," Clay reminded him with a smug smile. "I'll see you in a few," Clay added with a wink, before leaning close. "We still have some talking to do," Clay said in a deep, rich tone that made Evan shiver. Once Clay had left, Evan carried Nicky into the kitchen, putting some bread in the toaster for him.

"Did Clay have a sleepover?" Nicky asked when Evan set him down to butter the toast before sprinkling some cinnamon sugar on it.

"He slept on the sofa," Evan explained, cutting the bread down the middle.

"Why?" Nicky asked, watching Evan as he carried the plate to the table. Evan poured him a glass of apple juice, and Nicky climbed into one of the chairs.

"Because he was worried about you being sick," Evan answered, realizing that Clay had really stayed for Evan. Retrieving his cup, Evan joined Nicky at the table. Nicky ate and talked all about the hospital the night before, going on and on, but Evan barely heard him, his mind centering on Clay.

"Daddy," Nicky asked something, and Evan pulled his attention out of his mental wanderings. "Was I a big boy at the scary hospital?"

"Yes, you were," Evan reassured him. "You were a very big boy, and I was so proud of you." Evan hugged his son as Nicky finished the first half of his toast. "Why don't you finish eating, okay? When Clay gets back, I have to give you your medicine."

Nicky made a nasty face.

"You don't have to eat it. It's breathing medicine. All you have to do is sit on my lap while I hold the nebulizer near your face."

"No yucky stuff?" Nicky asked, scrunching his face in disbelief.

Evan chuckled and said, "No yucky stuff." Nicky finished eating, and Evan helped him wash up and brush his teeth. As they were finishing, the apartment door opened and closed. Evan made Nicky finish before letting him hurry away. As he cleaned up the bathroom and got dressed, he heard Nicky and Clay talking in the living room. He couldn't hear what they were saying, but he did hear Nicky giggling for a few seconds. After hanging up the towels, he walked back into the living room, setting up the nebulizer before putting in the dose of medication. Positioning Nicky on his lap, he turned on the machine and held the mister near Nicky's mouth and nose. "Just lay back and relax, okay?"

Nicky nodded, and Evan felt him almost sink into his embrace. This had to be the best feeling in the world, simply holding his son. Clay sat in a nearby chair, watching them. "You know you're wonderful with him."

"Thanks," Evan said with a smile, unsure of how else to respond. "I love him, more than I thought it was possible to love another person." Evan saw Nicky look up at him, and he nodded reassuringly before kissing his forehead. He wanted to say more, but stopped himself; he'd already said plenty the last time they were together.

"Evan, I wanted to tell you some things when we were alone, but it seems you're never alone, so I have to tell you this now." Clay slid to the edge of the chair, and Evan felt his hand slide along his arm. "I love you, Evan, and I think I always have. I just needed to pull my head out of my—" Clay looked at Nicky and stopped. "Well, you get the picture."

"Yeah, I think I do. But is this what you really want? I've had what I wanted most and lost it once—I don't think I could do that again." Evan felt his heart pounding in his chest, but he almost refused to let himself believe it. "Are you sure you're ready to admit to everyone that you're gay and in love with another man?"

"I already came out to my family a few weeks ago. They weren't really surprised. My mom said she'd been waiting for me to wake up for quite some time, and it seems like I finally have."

Evan peered down and saw Nicky looking up at him curiously, and Evan soothed his hand down his arm, feeling his son relax against him once more.

Clay took Evan's free hand in his. "I know you're finding this hard to believe, but there are a number of things I've decided, and the most important one is that I love you more than anyone else on earth. I've loved you almost since the day you walked into my dorm room, looking at me through huge lost-puppy eyes. You're my best friend and the best man I've ever known in my life, and if you'll have me, I'll spend the rest of my life trying to make you happy."

Evan found himself stunned into silence. This was the last thing he'd ever expected to happen. "You're serious, aren't you?" It was too much to hope for. How many times had he wished for Clay to tell him how he felt and that he loved him? Nicky began to squirm, and Evan soothed him, making sure the nebulizer was in the proper location before returning his attention to Clay. Evan found himself staring into those beautiful brown eyes, the same ones he'd fantasized about for almost as long as he could remember. "It's almost too good to believe," Evan said, looking down again at Nicky, whose eyes now appeared to be getting heavy. Evan listened quietly, Nicky's breathing again becoming much easier.

Turning off the machine, Evan got to his feet and slowly carried Nicky to his room. Evan turned back the comforter, and Nicky scooted under the covers, already half asleep. Evan looked around before going to his room and finding Nicky's bunny. Returning to his son's room, he handed the bunny to Nicky, who curled up into a ball, his eyes closed. Kissing his forehead, Evan left the door cracked as he walked to rejoin Clay in the living room.

"Is he asleep?" Clay asked, patting the sofa next to him.

"Yeah," Evan sighed, sitting next to Clay. "I understand how he feels. I didn't sleep much last night myself, although I felt better having you here. Sort of like old times."

"I meant what I said earlier, Ev," Clay told him softly, a hand sliding along his cheek. "I'd forgotten what you felt like against my skin." Clay leaned closer, and Evan blinked, not sure this was really happening. "A month ago, you gave me one hell of a kiss."

"I shouldn't have done that," Evan said, not really believing it.

"Yes, you should have—it helped make me realize just what I'd been missing." Clay stopped moving, and Evan could feel him looking deep into his eyes. "Passion, true feeling, and love." Evan felt Clay's hand slip around the back of his head, skin warm and soft on his neck. "You reminded me of what I want, and that's you." Clay moved closer and kissed him. A month earlier, Evan had kissed Clay almost out of desperation, but this was so different, softer and slower. He could really taste Clay and savor the warm softness against his own lips. His eyes slipping closed, Evan let himself float on the long-suppressed feelings he had for the man kissing him, moving closer to him, now holding him.

Clay's tongue teased its way along Evan's lip, and Evan moaned, lips parting in invitation as Clay held him closer, kissing him harder. "Clay, what if Nicky...?"

Backing away, Clay peered at him through half-lidded eyes. "If you want me to stop, all you have to do is say so."

Evan listened for any sound from the other side of the apartment, but heard nothing except the beating of his own heart pounding in his ears. Turning his eyes to Clay, Evan felt as though he were being drawn forward. This time he kissed Clay, his control snapping as he feasted on his lips. Body tingling, Evan kept kissing, feeling what felt like falling, but it was Clay pressing him back against the cushions, his weight on top of him, arms holding him, lips kissing, their bodies sharing their heat.

Clutching Clay's back, Evan arched into the touch, wanting Clay as close as possible, touching him in every way possible. Gasping for air, Evan broke the kiss only long enough to gulp air before returning to the bruising kisses they shared.

Evan felt his vision start to blur as their kissing continued. Clay's warm hands slid under his shirt, and Evan groaned as fingers found their way to a nipple, plucking the sensitive bud. Evan nearly cried out, but forced himself quiet, biting his lip as Clay's lips moved to his neck, licking and kissing the sensitive skin.

Fingers moved to the other nipple, pinching lightly as Evan gasped for breath and control of his own body. This was what he'd been wanting ever since the one night he'd had with Clay, and his body felt as though it were starved for affection. "Clay, I'm not going to be able control myself much longer," Evan moaned softly, and Clay chose that moment to slide his hand down Evan's chest, slipping his fingers beneath his waistband, and Evan did his best to swallow his groan as Clay continued teasing him. "Clay, I'm serious."

Lips came so close he could feel their heat. "I don't want you to control yourself. I want to see what I do to you." Clay kissed him again. "How you react to me." He felt Clay opening his belt, parting his pants with a tug. He'd dreamed of this, imagined it for years, and now it was coming true. He felt Clay's hands on his chest, sliding around him to his back, hands slipping into his pants, palms cupping his butt, pressing them closer. Through the layers of fabric, he could feel Clay's excitement pressing against his.

"Clay, please," Evan breathed, kissing Clay's neck as he gripped and pulled Clay's shirt up. He needed to feel him, touch him. Clay knelt over him, eyes dark as he pulled off his shirt before working open Evan's shirt buttons. The fabric parted and Clay resumed his kissing, their chests pressing together, skin to skin. Clay's hands again slipped under him, palms and fingers once again against his butt. "Want more, Clay, need more," Evan implored, and Clay pressed harder, their bodies melding, their minds losing themselves in one another. "Oh, Clay, I've wanted this for so long, you here with me."

"I know, Ev, and I'm sorry it took me so long to figure it all out," Clay told him through clenched teeth as Evan found a great spot at the base of Clay's neck, worrying it with his tongue. He could barely keep any semblance of control as Clay found one of his nipples with his lips.

"Clay!"

A loud knock on the door broke through his passion-induced haze, and Evan groaned, his body stilling as the knock came again. Clay groaned softly, and Evan felt his weight disappear. Hastily, Evan buttoned his shirt while Clay pulled his back over his head. Looking moderately respectable again, Evan walked to the door as the knocking sounded again, opening it slowly. The Ice Queen stood in the hallway, glaring at Evan as he peered out. "Clay is here, isn't he?" she accused rather than asked.

"Excuse me?" Evan responded, taken aback by her abruptness and definitely more than a little surprised. *Why did she have to show up now?* The few times he'd met her, Sheila had been intense and driven, but now she looked like the ice bitch from hell in her severe business suit and hair pulled so tight, her face looked stretched. Evan turned to look at Clay and then back at Sheila, wondering how he could just get her to go away.

"I tried his place, but he wasn't there, so I figured he was here. I need to talk to Clay." Stepping forward, she pressed the door open, walking inside and straight to where Clay stood near the sofa. "What is wrong with you?" she asked Clay.

"Sheila," Evan interrupted, "I'd appreciate it if you didn't wake Nicky."

"Who's Nicky?" she continued, even louder. "What, you two have another man? You are both sick." She turned back to Clay. "It's bad enough you cancelled our engagement for him, but you weren't happy with that either? You had to find someone besides him too?" Her voice kept getting louder.

"Sheila, that's enough! You'll wake Nicky. And I don't have to explain anything to you in my own home and neither does he." Evan glared at her. "So take your Ice Queen ass and leave."

Sheila gaped at him, saying nothing more, and Clay smirked for a second before putting his hand over his mouth. "Sheila," Clay said calmly, "why are you here? I thought we'd talked all this out the other day."

"I wanted to talk some sense into you, but I see that really isn't possible," Sheila answered, crossing her arms as she glared at Clay.

Evan could hardly believe this was happening or that he was going to say this, but he opened his mouth to speak. "Why don't you two sit down and talk. I'm going to check on Nicky." Evan motioned toward the table, and Sheila pulled out a chair, checking it over before deigning to sit.

"Are you sure?" Clay asked him.

"It's fine. You need to talk this out, and I need to make sure Nicky's okay." Evan walked toward Nicky's room, but turned before going too far out of earshot and said, "Just get her out of here before she starts frosting the windows."

Clay had the decency to roll his eyes and not laugh. Evan heard the chair slide out and then voices as the two of them began to talk. Evan desperately wanted to know what they were saying, but Nicky was more important. Pushing open his door, Evan peered inside. Nicky looked to be waking up, and Evan stepped to the bed, rubbing Nicky's back as he opened his eyes.

"Are you feeling better?" Evan asked, gazing down at his son. He knew the adoption hadn't gone through yet, and he lived in fear that some family member would come forward and decide they wanted Nicky, but so far that hadn't happened. Evan had surprised himself with just how fast he'd begun to think of Nicky as his son. In a matter of days, he'd wondered what his life would be like without him, and now he couldn't picture it any other way. Brushing his hand over Nicky's forehead, he felt cool, dry skin under his palm and breathed a sigh of relief. "You feel better," Evan said, as Nicky squirmed to get out of bed.

"Is Clay still here?" Nicky asked excitedly.

"Yes, he's out talking with the Ice Queen."

Nicky's eyes widened. Bounding off the bed, Nicky hurried to the door, pulling it open. Evan followed, catching up to Nicky in the living room, his mouth hanging open. "Daddy," he asked, turning back to Evan, "Where's her crown?" Nicky turned back to Sheila, pointing. "Won't she melt?"

Evan glanced at Clay, who tried to cover his laughter, while Sheila simply looked sour. Evan, slightly embarrassed, tried to change the subject. "Let's get you cleaned up and dressed." Taking Nicky's hand, he led him back to the bedroom with Nicky craning his head as if to see if Sheila would freeze and turn completely white.

In the bathroom, Evan ran Nicky a bath, and Nicky stripped off his pajamas. Dumping his bath toys in the tub, he climbed in and began scooting submarines under the water and motorboats along the side of the tub, of course making all the appropriate sounds. "Daddy, how long is the Ice Queen going to stay?"

"Not long," he answered, letting Nicky play, thinking about what she and Clay could be talking about. Granted, they'd been engaged for a while, but they'd been living apart for a while, too, and they couldn't be very close any longer. Evan shook his head to clear away those thoughts. Evan didn't like Sheila, but that didn't mean she didn't have feelings. At least they were talking.

"Is Clay going to sleep over again?"

"I don't know," Evan answered Nicky as he filled a plastic motorboat with water and it sank to the bottom of the tub. "Why don't you wash yourself and then I'll wash your hair for you."

Once Nicky was clean, Evan held out a bath sheet. Nicky stepped into it, and Evan held him close before helping Nicky dry himself. There was a soft knock on the door, and Evan answered, "Yes, Clay." Clay peered into the room. "Is she gone?"

"Yes," Clay answered.

"We'll be done here in a few minutes." Evan told him, and Clay closed the door again.

Evan swept Nicky off his feet, towel and all, carrying him airplane-style into his room. "Go ahead and get dressed. Bring me your shoes when you're done, and I'll help you tie them."

"Okay," Nicky said, hurrying to his dresser, pulling out the drawers to get his clothes. Evan watched for a few seconds before returning to the bathroom to clean up the mess.

After finishing in the bathroom, Evan shut off the lights, walking to the living area. "Everything okay?" Evan asked as he found Clay sitting on the sofa looking like he'd been waiting for him.

Clay sighed. "She's hurt, and I can't really blame her. I led her on for a long time, and she's a little shocked."

Evan sat next to him. "I can see that," Evan said, "but you're both better off being honest with each other."

Clay chuckled. "You sound like Father Val used to, remember?" Evan nodded, but he didn't say anything. "Lately I've been thinking a lot about our time in school together."

"Me too," Evan echoed, listening for Nicky. "You don't think we're trying to recapture or relive our youth do you?"

"I don't know about you," Clay said, grinning as he tugged Evan close to him, "but I didn't even dream I'd get to do this back then. I also never thought you'd have a kid or that I'd be so incredibly happy about it." Evan felt Clay kiss behind his ear. "No, this is better than what we had when we were kids, because I know I love you now, and I don't intend to let you go."

Little feet hurried toward them, with Nicky launching himself onto the sofa, landing with his body on Evan's lap and his legs on Clay's. "Someone's feeling better," Clay observed, and Nicky giggled as Clay tickled him.

"You need to take it easy," Evan scolded both of them, as he lifted Nicky onto his lap. "Remember you were at the hospital last night, and you don't want to have to go back." Nicky shook his head. "Then you can watch television for a while, but only if you're quiet. Okay?"

"Okay, Daddy." Nicky slipped off Evan's lap, turning on the television before settling onto the floor. Evan got up and retrieved a blanket, lifting Nicky off the floor so he could slip it beneath him before settling back onto the sofa next to Clay, who immediately pulled him close.

"If I'm going to watch *Sesame Street*, I at least get to hold you," Clay whispered into Evan's ear, and right then, Evan didn't care what was on television, or about much else at all. Nicky's voice rang through the room as he sang along with the television characters, and Evan shared a smile with Clay, resting his head against his love's shoulder.

"I waited a long time for this, you know," Evan told Clay softly.

Clay squeezed him a little tighter. "What?"

"This—someone to just sit and be with." Evan turned to look into Clay's eyes. "I thought I had it once before, but…."

"You have it now, Ev," Clay told him softly. "Who knows you better than me? I've known you forever, and I love you for you." Clay leaned close, kissing him lightly.

"Eww, kissing," Nicky said from the floor, big eyes looking up at them. Evan smiled, shaking his head slowly, but said nothing, the smile on his face all he needed.

Lunch, the afternoon, and a quiet dinner all passed in quiet harmony. Evan gave Nicky his medicine in the afternoon and put him down for a nap that lasted a couple of hours. He and Clay spent part of that time making out on the sofa, but half the time Evan kept listening for another knock on the door and the rest he was listening for Nicky, so mostly, Clay held him, arms tight around his chest, as they watched an old movie. Dinner was macaroni and cheese and Nicky's favorite, chicken nuggets. After making dinner and cleaning up, Evan collapsed on the sofa, the lack of sleep the night before definitely catching up with him. A knock on the door made Evan jump; he'd had enough surprises today. Getting up with a groan, he cracked the door, seeing Wendy peering back at him. "Is everything okay?" she asked.

Evan opened the door. "Yeah, come on in."

Nicky ran up behind him, giving Wendy a hug. "I went to the hospital, and they gave me a ride in the bed, and took pictures of my guts," Nicky told her excitedly, and Evan wondered where all this excitement was when it had been happening.

"Wendy, this is Clay. I think you met a while ago," Evan said, making introductions.

"I believe we did, a while ago," Wendy said, extending her hand. "It's nice to see you again. Evan has told me a lot about you." They shook hands, and she turned back to Evan. "I didn't mean to disturb you, but I wanted to make sure this guy," she said, ruffling Nicky's hair, "was all right."

"They think it was just a virus, and as you can see, he seems to be doing much better." Evan lifted Nicky into his arms. "Although I think it's time for your medicine before you go to bed."

Nicky made a face, and the adults chuckled. "I'll see you later, then," Wendy said, moving toward the door. "I'm glad you're feeling better," she added to Nicky, giving him a belly tickle before closing the door behind her.

"She seems very nice," Clay commented once the door was closed.

Evan felt himself yawn, and seeing Nicky yawn as well, Evan used the opportunity to get him into his pajamas. Sitting in the chair in his room, Evan turned on the nebulizer for Nicky's medication before putting him into bed. "Would you read me a story?" Nicky asked, tucked under light covers.

"Which one would you like?" Nicky handed him a book, and Evan opened it and began to read. "Peter Rabbit...." Nicky fell asleep before he was halfway through, and Evan found himself yawning as he cracked the door on his way out.

"I think I'm going to bed as well," Evan said. He'd been wondering all day what would happen now. Would Clay stay? He wanted him to.

Clay got up from the sofa, turning off the lights in the living room. "Ev, do you want me to go?"

He shook his head, holding out his hand. Clay's hand slipped into his, and Evan led him through the dark apartment to his bedroom. Closing the door behind them, Evan stared into the darkness. "Do you remember the last time we were together like this?"

Arms encircled Evan's waist, tugging him close. "Uh-huh. I was so scared you'd send me away. That you weren't interested in me as anything other than a friend." Clay's hot breath slid over his neck, and Evan felt himself shiver with excitement. "I found out how wrong I was that night, and my track record hasn't been much better since," Clay murmured.

"I think you're about to make up for that," Evan answered as Clay's lips found his neck, tongue slicking along his skin. Evan moaned softly, holding on to Clay's back to steady his already shaking legs. Clay kept working on his skin, and Evan found his fingers winding through Clay's soft hair, holding him as his neck and back stretched into the sensations, silently begging for more. The lips slipped away, and Evan heard nothing, the room silent except for his own deep breathing.

The small lamp on his dresser snapped on, and Evan blinked into the soft light. "The last time we were together, I couldn't see," Clay explained as he stalked back toward him, "and this time I definitely plan to see all of you." Clay took his mouth in a deep, hard kiss that took Evan's breath away. Pressing him backward, Clay's weight tipped his balance, and they tumbled onto the bed, Clay's lips never leaving his.

This was what Evan had dreamed about for years. Clay, his Clay, was making love to him. He'd gotten a taste all those years ago, and he was more than ready for seconds. Evan returned every kiss, feasting on Clay's mouth, his hands clutching the fabric of Clay's shirt, pulling it up and away, tearing his lips away only long enough to get Clay's shirt off before attacking him again. Clay's hands worked open the buttons of Evan's shirt. The fabric parted, and their chests pressed together. Clay felt different to Evan, the sparse hair of his youthful chest replaced by a pelt of soft, dark curls that tickled his own smooth skin. Letting his hands roam, Evan compared the feel of Clay's skin against his to what he remembered, and the memories paled in comparison. Clay had been an attractive teenager, but he was a spectacular man. Strong arms pulled Evan close, tightening around his waist, as Clay's lips found his sensitive nipples, and Evan squirmed with delight in the tight embrace. "Clay." Evan's voice quivered, and Clay's dark eyes shifted upward, meeting Evan's.

"Do you want me to stop?" Clay asked wickedly.

"No," Evan answered, thrusting his chest forward, "don't stop."

"Not until you tell me," Clay breathed, air flowing over Evan's damp skin. Hands and lips roamed over his chest, Clay's weight pressing him against the bed. Holding his breath, Evan felt Clay's hands slide down his stomach, fingers tickling just above his waistband before opening his belt, parting the fabric of his pants. "I seem to remember we were here earlier," Clay teased softly, a hand holding Evan's shoulders to the mattress while the other stroked him through the fabric.

Evan desperately wanted to see what Clay was doing, but he couldn't. All he could do was feel and let the sensations of Clay's hands on his skin wash over him. Clay's hands slid into his underwear, fingers cupping him, and Evan held his breath, body stretching, anticipating what Clay would do next. Evan felt Clay's weight shift, and he realized he was no longer being touched. Sitting up to see what was happening, Clay stood between his legs, pulling his pants down his legs. "Let's get you naked," Clay told him. "I want to see all of you." Evan's pants slipped off, and Clay dropped them on the floor. Evan squirmed out of his shirt and watched as Clay opened his own pants, sliding them down his legs.

Clay stood just out of reach, looking at him with an expression bordering on awe, while Evan feasted his own eyes on Clay. Wide shoulders, narrow hips, strong, corded legs. Clay stepped toward him, and Evan felt his mouth go dry and his breath hitch. Clay stepped closer, and Evan felt himself move under his lover's gaze as though he were talking to him, telling him to lie back on the bed. When he felt the pillow under his head, Evan felt Clay's gaze move closer, and he felt Clay's legs slide against his. Almost too stunned to move, Evan held himself still as Clay moved over him, legs, then hips, chest, and finally hands, touching him. Every inch of his skin felt as though it were on fire, and when Clay's lips touched him again, he clutched Clay's back, pressing up against him, undulating. Lifting his head, Clay smoothed his hand down Evan's cheek.

"I want you, Clay. I've waited a long time, and I want you so bad," Evan told Clay, his voice breaking as he clutched him, legs wrapping around Clay's waist.

"Ev," Clay breathed, "it's been a long time for me, about seven years."

Evan stilled before kissing Clay hard. He loved that Clay hadn't been with another guy since him. "You've never done *this* before?" Evan asked softly, and Clay shook his head. "Just use your fingers," Evan said, moving his gaze to the bedside table. Clay reached for the small bottle, snapping it open before slicking his fingers.

"I don't want to hurt you," Clay said softly.

"You won't—you couldn't," Evan answered, stilling when he felt Clay's fingers slide along his crease and against his opening, then a finger slowly pressed into his body and Evan hissed, pulling Clay into a hard kiss that nearly drew blood. "That's it, now take it easy," Evan told him, breathing in deep before asking Clay to add a second finger. Clay got the hang of things fast, watching him as he moved his fingers in and out of Evan's body. Reaching to the nightstand, Evan handed Clay a condom. "Just go slow."

Clays fingers withdrew, and Evan waited until he felt Clay press against him, Evan's body opening as his lover pressed inside. Evan couldn't stop a smile passing his lips when he saw the look of sheer and utter amazement on Clay's face as their bodies joined together for the first time. Evan felt Clay moving inside him, touching him in a way no one else had ever done. With every move, Evan felt his heart reach to Clay, and his reaching back, and when they touched, Evan felt his body react, climaxing between their bodies as he felt Clay still, crying out against his lips.

Pulling his lover to him, Evan held Clay until their bodies separated. Slowly, Clay lifted himself off the bed, and Evan heard him walk to the bathroom, returning with a towel. Clay's gentle touch wiped him clean, and then the towel joined their clothes on the floor, and the light went out. Bed dipping, Evan moved to let Clay in next to him, and strong arms tugged him close. "I love you, Evan. I think I always have."

"I love you too."

"Can I ask you something?" Clay asked, and Evan nodded his answer against his skin. "Where do we go from here?"

Evan rolled over, his arms snaking around Clay's neck. "We take it one day at a time and see where the journey leads us." Evan felt his eyes close as he held onto Clay, wondering if this was for real and just how long it would last. He wanted it to be forever, but that was probably too much for him to hope for.

Chapter 7

"NICKY, if you don't hurry, we're going to be late!" Evan called up the stairs, and waited until he heard the thumping sound of booted feet on the hallway floor, followed by the clomp of heavy treads on the stairs. "Have you got everything? You're not going to be able to call me to bring your gym shoes in to school if you forget," Evan added with a smile.

Nicky rolled his eyes in dramatic fashion, as only a teenager can. "I packed everything you laid out for me, even the uncool stuff."

"You mean like underwear?" Evan snapped back, referring to his son's tendency lately to go commando. Since he did the laundry, Evan had been curious as to why there was nothing of that particular article of clothing to be washed.

"You know, Dad, but I always wondered why you weren't like other parents. You talk about everything, even the stuff other kids' folks hide from. I always wondered what it would be like to have a dad who didn't talk about my underwear." Evan saw a gleam form in Nicky's eyes. "Or ask if I knew how to use condoms. By the way, the banana thing was just gross," Nicky added as he shuddered exaggeratedly. Nicky stepped closer, the smirk on his lips turning to a smile. "Or a dad who when I was thirteen asked me if I like boys or girls and told me either one was okay as long as I was true to myself. God, that was embarrassing."

Nicky jumped back as Evan took a good-natured swipe at his son. Nicky dropped his bag and took off through the hall and into the kitchen with Evan right behind him, both of them laughing. "Damn, you can move for an old man," Nicky teased as Evan caught him.

"Get your stuff in the car," he chuckled, before adding, "and someday you'll appreciate just how good you have it." Evan opened a cupboard, pulling out a box of his athletic son's favorite snack, cinnamon granola bars. "Put these in your backpack too."

Nicky took them and smiled. "Thanks, Dad," he said as he took the box. Evan stared at his son as though he were memorizing his face—it would be awhile before he saw it again. Turning away, he hid his reaction to the lump forming in his throat by turning on the tap to get a drink.

Hearing those boots on the floor, Evan stared out of the kitchen window into the small backyard. The area where Nicky's swing set had been was now planted with shrubs, the wooden structure having been given away years ago. Releasing his held breath, Evan dumped the rest of the water in his glass down the drain before walking back through the house and up the stairs to make sure Nicky hadn't forgotten anything.

In Nicky's room, he looked near the unmade bed and checked around the closet before satisfying himself that Nicky had gotten everything. Stopping at the door, he looked back into the room, a telltale mixture of the boy he'd been and the young man his Nicky had become. Most of the room looked nothing like the small apartment bedroom Nicky had had when Evan had first brought him home, but on the corner of the dresser stood a lamp in the shape of a sailboat, along with trophies and God knew what else.

A moose clomped up the stairs, or at least what sounded like a moose, and Evan turned from the room. "You ready, Dad?"

Evan nodded, closing the door behind him as he followed Nicky down the stairs. He couldn't help stopping at a photograph of Nicky and himself on the beach playing in the sand that first summer he'd brought him home. Evan felt the memories wash over him, nearly threatening to carry him away. Swallowing hard again, he forced himself to move on and not look at any of the other pictures or he'd be bawling his eyes out before they made it to the car.

At the bottom of the stairs, he picked up Nicky's last box, carrying it out and placing it in the trunk. "I locked the door and checked it," Nicky told him as he hurried by. "Can I drive?"

The very thought sent a chill through him. "No."

"I'll have my permit next year," he teased, and Evan fixed him with a stare.

"More like two years, and when you do, I'll take my life in my hands and help you learn to drive, but until that time, I don't have a death wish," Evan quipped as he climbed into the car. That had to be every parent's nightmare—their kid learning to drive. Evan noticed that Nicky stopped to look at the house before getting in the car and closing the door. Evan started the car while Nicky got his seat belt on. As they pulled away from the house, Nicky fiddled with the radio, tuning it to some god-awful station, the sounds rattling Evan's back teeth. When Nicky was done, Evan simply pushed a button and the station returned to something that didn't make Evan want to jab his ears with an ice pick to make it stop.

"Dad, that was a cool station."

"It had to be, and my ears were bleeding after two seconds," he retorted with a grin and saw Nicky pull out his iPod. He could live with that, but he fixed him with a glare anyway.

"I know, I won't turn it up too loud." Nicky rolled his eyes. "You're worse than an old lady," he quipped before his mouth softened. Settling back in his seat, Nicky listened to his music while Evan turned the car onto the freeway for the ride north. He remembered taking this same ride along the same route with Father Val years before. The city extended farther out, but soon they were passing through fields and rolling hills. He barely remembered his trip with Father Val, but those impressions stayed with him somehow.

"Nicky," Evan called, and he saw his son remove the buds from his ears, "I need to talk to you about something."

"Can't it wait, Dad?" Nicky whined, but he turned off his music, and Evan shut off the radio.

"No, it can't," Evan said with a swallow. "I know you're fourteen and think you know everything about the world, but there are things I've kept from you, things that you should know." God, he'd never wanted to have this talk with Nicky, but he felt he had to. "Do you know why I became a teacher?"

"You're not a teacher; you're a principal," Nicky corrected with a proud smile.

"Yes, but do you know why I went into education?"

Nicky looked at him, cocking his head slightly. "No, I guess I thought you liked it."

"I do, but there's something else, and you should know this for your own protection. Back when I was at St. Bart's, one of the instructors used his influence to...." Evan looked back at the road, trying to figure out how to tell his son what had happened to him. He didn't want to scare him, but he also didn't want anything to happen to him. "Nicky, I was abused by a teacher." Evan took a deep breath. "The details aren't important, and he's no longer at the school. But I want you to promise you'll tell me if anyone approaches you that way or if you hear about that happening to someone else." The look on Nicky's face made Evan wish he'd never said anything.

155

"And you're letting me go there?"

"It wasn't the school, it was one person, and I'm not telling you to frighten you. I just want you to be aware so it doesn't happen to you or anyone else. That's why I became a teacher, and now a principal, because I never want that to happen to another young person if I can help it," Evan told his son. "I know this is not pleasant to think about."

"Someone hurt you?" Nicky asked, his eyes wide, tinged with a touch of fear.

"Yes, so if anything ever happens, or you think someone is being hurt by a teacher or another student, tell Father Val right away. He'll know exactly what to do."

"I can't narc, Dad," Nicky told him, giving him another of those "duh" looks. "Did you narc on the teacher? Is that why he's no longer at the school?"

"No," Evan answered. "He's no longer at the school because the last time he tried something, I sort of made sure he couldn't walk right for a very long time."

"Way to go, Dad," Nicky said with a grin and a fist pump. "Don't worry, no one's gonna do anything to me." Evan stared at his son with one of his stern principal looks, knowing it was the one way to wear him down. "Okay, Dad, I promise if something happens, I'll tell you."

"Good, because you're my son, and I never want anything bad to happen to you," Evan told him, and Nicky put his earbuds back in his ears before turning his iPod back on, taking them off a few minutes later.

"Did other bad stuff happen to you? I mean, besides having your parents die, like mine did."

"Yes," Evan answered truthfully, "and I promise I'll tell you all about it when you're older."

Nicky seemed to accept that answer, his attention disappearing behind his earbuds, and Evan drove in quiet contemplation, recognizing a number of the landmarks as they got close to the school. At the first sight of the main building, Evan saw the tower and then the rest of the school perched on its hilltop. It looked the same from here, and for a few seconds Evan found himself transported back to the first time he'd seen the building with Father Val. He knew now he'd simply been scared, but then it had felt like so much more.

As they got closer, Nicky pulled off his earbuds, putting the iPod away. "See that slope?" Evan asked, pointing. "We used to sled down that in the winter, and over there is the orchard, and there's the lawn where we used to throw footballs or play Frisbee on sunny days."

"I know, Dad. You told me when we toured the school last spring." Nicky exaggeratedly rolled his eyes. "And over there is where you flew the helicopter."

Pulling closer, Evan turned up the drive, the car climbing the hill, riding past the cemetery, continuing their journey to the parking lot at the top of the hill. Getting out, Evan inhaled deeply, memories flooding back. Looking toward the dorm building, he half expected to see his seventeen-year-old self come rushing out with Dex, Frankie, Peter, and Patrick.

"Dad, are you going to spend all day walking down memory lane or are you gonna help me unload?" Evan looked around and found Nicky already standing by the trunk, waiting for him. Popping it open, he pulled out a suitcase, leading the way toward the dorm.

Inside, not much had changed, and Evan led the way to the freshman floor where a brother waited with a clipboard. "Nicolas Donaldson," Nicky told him.

"Yes, you're in room fifteen, down the hall on your right," he said, pointing. "I'm the floor supervisor, if you have any questions or need anything, please let me know."

"Thank you," Nicky answered, hurrying to his room while Evan watched.

"Can I help you?" the brother asked him.

"Brother Timothy?" Evan asked, a smile bursting onto his face. "Sorry," Evan said, putting down the suitcase. "I'm Evan Donaldson. I went to school here, oh, I guess it's eighteen years ago."

"Evan." He seemed to search his memory before a smile lit his face. "Oh my goodness, I never would have guessed. And Nicolas is your son?"

"Yes, I adopted him when he was four," Evan answered. "Excuse me," he said, seeing Nicky poke his head out of his room, "I'm being called. It was good to see you," Evan added as he carried Nicky's suitcase down the hall. At the room, he heard Nicky's excited voice and that of another boy, both of them chattering away about bands and groups that meant nothing to Evan but had the teenagers all in a tizzy. "I've got your suitcase," Evan said, setting it by the door.

"Thanks, Dad. Could you bring in the rest of my stuff from the car?" Nicky asked without even looking at him.

"What do you think I am—your pack mule? Get up and bring in your own stuff," Evan retorted, glaring at his son, shaking his head.

"I'll help you," the other boy said, getting up, both boys hurrying down the hall, talking to beat the band.

"Looks like they became friends in a hurry." Evan turned around to see a plump, short woman standing behind him. "I'm Romona Peters, and the boy with your son is my son Eddie. I was worried he'd have trouble making friends, but they seem to be doing just fine."

Evan nodded slowly, watching where the boys disappeared out the door. "I'm Evan Donaldson, and that was my son Nicky." He looked back at her. "I believe you're right—they're going to be fine, and they probably don't need our help. Would you like to get a cup of coffee?"

She smiled up at him. "That would be nice," Romona answered, and Evan motioned her in the right direction. "The cafeteria's out this door and just down the walk."

"Have you been here before?" she asked as they reached the stairs.

"I went to school here," he told her. "That was a while ago, but it looks like things haven't changed much." They made their way outside and across the sidewalk. Pulling open the doors, they found a table with cookies and an urn of coffee. Pouring a cup, he joined Romona and a few of the other parents at a table.

"So, Mr. Donaldson, where's Nicky's mother?" Romona asked innocently.

"Nicky's parents died when he was young, and I adopted him," Evan explained, figuring it wasn't necessary to go into all the details about his and Nicky's life.

"How old was he?"

Evan smiled. "Four. When I got him, his parents had been killed in an accident a few weeks earlier. He was the most adorable boy I'd ever seen." Evan knew he'd remember that day for the rest of his life, for so many reasons. The conversation changed tracks, and Evan relaxed, talking and chatting with the other parents until they started to get up and move away. Most had much longer drives than he did and needed to get back on the road. Evan said goodbye before he and Romona made their way back up to their boys' room. The two were unpacking, talking up a storm, and Evan doubted either of them knew their parents had left in the first place.

Romona was saying her goodbyes, and Evan left the room, dragging Nicky with him, to give her and her son a few minutes together. "I'm going to see Father Val, but I'll stop by before I leave."

"No sweat, Dad. Eddie's really cool. I think this is going to be a great place," Nicky said, breaking into a huge smile. Not that Evan had been worried, but it was reassuring to see Nicky getting along already. Nicky went back in the room as soon as Romona came out, wiping her eyes with a tissue before saying goodbye.

Taking another peek into the room, Evan walked down the hall and down the stairs closest to the academic building. Outside, Evan stopped on the walk, watching boys already throwing a football. No matter how many times Dex had tried to show him, that was one thing he'd never gotten the hang of—throwing a spiral. As he stood, Evan felt someone stand next to him. "That brings back memories," Evan said softly.

"Boys have been playing on that patch of grass for over a century now." Evan knew that voice. Turning, he found himself looking into a very familiar set of eyes.

"Father Val," Evan said. He looked older, and there were wrinkles around his eyes, but they were as clear and sharp as he remembered. "I was just coming to see you." Evan waited a few seconds before supplying, "I'm Evan."

Father Val's momentary confusion morphed into sheer delight. "My goodness, I was hoping I'd get a chance to see you. When I first got the application for your son, I didn't make the connection." Father Val began walking toward the building, and Evan followed along. "I guess I never expected you to have children."

Evan opened and held the door. "I adopted Nicky when he was four," he explained, and he followed the old priest inside and down the hallway. "His parents were killed the same way mine were."

Father Val paused for a second outside his door before pulling it open, and Evan walked inside. The office looked almost exactly the same as he remembered, and Evan sat in one of the old chairs, feeling the soft leather, now worn by generations of hands. "I understand you're the principal of your own school. Why isn't Nicky going there?"

"We talked it over and decided that there, he'd always be the principal's kid, but here, he'd be like everyone else. That was important. Besides, I made great friendships here, ones that have lasted my whole life. I still talk to Dex and Frankie, and some of the other guys I hear from occasionally."

"I don't know how to ask this, but what about Clay? The last day you were here, you asked me for advice, and I've always wondered if I steered you wrong."

"I thought you had for a long time, but no, you didn't," Evan said with a smile. "You were right. It took almost seven years, but Clay and I did find our way back to one another. Clay's a lawyer, and he helped me with the adoption, and after a bumpy road, we found each other again. We've been together ten of the happiest years of my life. And in some way, I owe it to you because I know if we'd have stayed together after high school, I wouldn't have him now. We both had a lot of growing up to do. We've raised Nicky together and built what I like to think is a great life for each other and him." Evan felt himself choking up. "We've loved each other and cared for each other for almost as long as I can remember, and in a lot of ways I have you to thank for that. For bringing me here," Evan said, looking around the office, "and giving me a chance at a life I'd given up on. I owe you a great deal."

Father Val stood up from behind his desk, walking around to where Evan sat. "You owe me and the school nothing. Yes, we gave you a home when you needed one, and I thank God every day that He brought you to us, but look what you've done with that gift."

Evan felt himself squirm under the old priest's gaze. "I don't understand."

"We gave you a home, and you gave others one as well. Look at your son. He's bright, and I dare say happy and healthy. We gave you a home, and you gave one to him. And let's not forget every student you've encouraged and helped over the years. I'll bet you never knew that Arthur Pinkus was also a student here a number of years before you and that I had him as a student when I was teaching. Once he became an educator, we talked often, and one day a number of years ago, he told he about hiring one of our graduates—'a brilliant mathematical mind', he called you. Said you could have done anything, but that you had a gift for teaching and knowing how to reach your students. You took the gift that God allowed us to give you and made lives better for other people, and will continue to do so long after the rest of us are gone. So, as I said, Evan, you owe us nothing."

Father Val fell silent, and Evan looked at him, wondering if he had more to say. "Is Clay here with you?"

Evan shook his head. "He wanted to come, but he had an appointment that was too important."

"More important than his son?" Father Val asked, sounding surprised.

"After Clay helped me adopt Nicky, his firm got a few more requests for adoption assistance, and Clay handled those as well." Evan sat up straighter as he thought of his Clay. "He's a child advocate attorney, and today he's helping another child find a good home. He and Nicky said their goodbyes this morning, and he'll be here for parents' day next month. Nicky made him promise." Evan found himself smiling as he looked around the office. "It's funny, but everywhere I look, I half expect to see all the people I knew when I was here." Evan's hands fidgeted in his lap, his thumbs rubbing together nervously.

"I get the feeling there's something else you want to ask."

"There is one thing I've wanted to know for quite a while, and I figured you would be the only one who might have an answer. I tried for years to block it out of my mind." Evan swallowed. "I've never told Nicky any of the details, though I've promised myself I will when he's older."

"He certainly won't hear it from any of us." Evan felt Father Val's hand touch his arm. "I've been teaching for going on forty years, and what happened to you is the one thing, above all, that I regret. I've prayed for guidance every single day since, and I've looked for any of the signs I overlooked with you. I regret that it happened and even more so that I didn't take action when you told me."

"I understand that and forgave you a long time ago. Holding on to hate and anger didn't help. It only made things worse. What I wanted to ask was if you knew what happened to Brother Renier. It's his face I saw in my nightmares and still do sometimes, although now they're nightmares about something happening to Nicky. It's always that man's face I see."

"Are you looking for vengeance of some kind? Because that's just as destructive as hate and anger."

"No, I think I'm simply looking for closure somehow," Evan said softly, not really sure what that meant or what he was even hoping to achieve by asking the question. For years he'd tried to put what had happened behind him, and for the most part he had. Evan had learned a long time ago that dwelling on the bad only made things worse, and he had many people in his life who filled his days with happiness. "In some ways, I wish I could just let this go, but after all these years, I know I can't, and I was hoping you might know something."

Father Val's expression betrayed nothing, and at first Evan figured he'd get nothing at all, but then he saw the priest sigh softly. "I must be careful with what I say, but after he left the school, Brother Renier traveled around a lot. Rumors followed him, and he wasn't able to find employment. I know he spent time in one of the monasteries in Europe. I'm told he prayed very hard over what he'd done and spent a number of years in self-imposed isolation."

Evan held back the scoff that threatened. The man was a pedophile. Evan doubted prayer alone was going to help him. Maybe intensive psychotherapy, but not much else.

Father Val sighed once again. "It's my understanding that Brother Renier deeply regretted his behavior and spent years trying to drive away his demons. I honestly cannot tell you if he was ever truly successful. But two years ago, he came to me, or more accurately, called me to him from his hospital bed. He had no place to go and needed care that he could no longer provide for himself. I went to see him and found out he had cancer. Since then, his condition has stabilized somewhat, but he'll never be able to care for himself again."

"So you do know where he is?" Evan inquired.

Father Val's eyes softened, and he inclined his head slightly. "Brother Renier is in the rectory."

Evan felt as though he'd been punched. He stared at Father Val in total disbelief. "He's here? What is that pedophilic monster doing this close to a school?" Evan stood up, walking toward the door. His first instinct was to get Nicky and get the hell out of here. There was no way his son was going to be anywhere near his one-time abuser.

"Evan." Father Val's voice projected a calm firmness Evan recognized. He used that same tone with his students. "Please sit down." Reluctantly, Evan sat on the edge of the chair, waiting for some explanation as he glared at the priest. "Brother Renier is bedridden and has been since he came here. He has no contact with any of the students whatsoever," Father Val added firmly. "He's one of the brothers, and as such we take care of each other, regardless of another man's sin. I would never have allowed him here if he posed any danger to any of our students. As far as I know, none of them have ever even seen him."

Some of Evan's anger dissipated. He still wasn't sure how happy he was having the man that close to Nicky, regardless of the circumstances. "He's...."

"Dying? Yes," Father Val supplied, and Evan couldn't say he was sorry for the man. He hoped it was truly painful. "Brother Renier is a sinner, we all are, and like the rest of us, he's going to die. His death will come sooner rather than later." Father Val stood up, and Evan did as well. "I hope you got some of what you were looking for and can find peace." Father Val held out his hand, and Evan shook it before leaving the office.

In the center of the building near the staircase, Evan looked up into the spirals that curved toward the roof. Taking a step onto the first stair, Evan found himself climbing upward to the second floor and down the hallway, pausing outside a classroom doorway. He knew this door and knew the room behind it. "Evan." Father Val's voice made him jump. He hadn't heard him come up behind him. "Would you like to see him?"

The words on the tip of his tongue were to say, "Hell no." He should simply turn and walk away, but he couldn't. His feet seemed rooted on the spot. Reaching forward, Evan opened the door, walking into the room. For a second Evan was seventeen again as a stab of fear overtook him. Then everything changed, and he saw the room for what it was, simply a classroom. The walls

165

had been painted, the desks in his memory gone, replaced with new ones. Evan saw that the old cabinets against the far wall were gone. Turning toward the back wall, Evan saw the closet doorway, but no door. Walking closer, he saw a pass-through with windows from both classrooms looking into what appeared to be a computer lab. "All the closets in the rooms were remodeled away shortly after you left. We now have windowed study rooms and computer labs," Father Val explained, placing a hand on his shoulder. "It also means that a teacher from one room can see into the next."

Evan turned, smiling slightly as a little more of the pain he'd carried all those years slipped away. That man couldn't hurt him anymore, and it was time he let go. "Yes." Evan looked into Father Val's eyes. "I'd like to see him," he said, the calmness in his voice surprising him, and Father Val nodded, leading them out of the room.

On the sunlit path leading toward the back of the property, Evan stopped, taking a deep breath of the crisp autumn air. "You don't have to do this," Father Val told him, but Evan knew otherwise. He *did* need to do this. Why, he really couldn't understand, he just knew he needed to see.

At the door of the rectory, Evan followed Father Val inside and down the hallway to the last room on the right. Evan peered inside. The small, darkened room contained a hospital bed, a table, and little else. The monks lived plainly, as was evident. A thin figure rested beneath the covers, eyes closed. Releasing a deep breath, Evan stepped into the room, watching as the man's eyes slid open, blinking at him. Evan didn't recognize anything about this man. He looked nothing like the man he remembered from his nightmares, yet when he looked into those eyes, he saw the same soul he remembered, and it sent a shiver down his spine. "Father Val?" the man asked in a voice barely above a whisper.

"Just someone to see you," Father Val answered softly. "He used to be a student here."

Brother Renier's gaze fell on Evan, and he stared back, meeting those eyes with a gaze that surprised him. This was his last chance to emotionally stand up to the man who'd tormented him, and he wasn't going to back down. "Do I know you?"

"You did, a long time ago," Evan answered, wondering what he expected to find by coming here. "I was one of your students."

"I don't remember you," Brother Renier said, lifting his head off the pillow for a brief second. He looked like little more than a skeleton covered with skin, cheeks hollow, all flesh and vitality faded away.

"I remember you, very well," Evan answered harshly, trying to decide how far to take this, until he realized it didn't matter. The man would be dead, and Evan would live, as would Clay and all the other people he loved. This man could hurt no one anymore. Age and disease had erased anything he might have been.

"We should go," Father Val prompted from the door. Saying no more, Evan turned away from the bed, looking to Father Val for a second and then back at Brother Renier.

"There's a special place in hell reserved for you," Evan said softly enough that only Brother Renier could hear him. Straightening up, Evan turned a final time, leaving the room and walking out of the building, back into the fresh air and sunshine. Gulping in the clean, cool air, Evan stretched as though he were waking from a long sleep. He heard Father Val walking up to him, footsteps crunching on the first leaves to fall. "Thank you," Evan said, turning to the man who'd rescued him from the streets and become as close to a father and mentor as anyone he'd had. "I'll see you for parents' day, and if you're in the city, please call. Clay and I would both love it if you'd visit."

Father Val nodded and extended his hand, but Evan stepped closer, embracing him in a hug. "I love you," he said softly, feeling the older man return his hug. Stepping away, Evan gave the priest a final smile before walking back toward the dormitory building.

As he got close to Nicky's room, Evan could hear boys talking a mile a minute, and when Evan peered inside, he saw a group of boys seated on the floor playing some sort of game with cards he didn't recognize. Evan smiled as Nicky took his turn and then set down his cards before getting to his feet. "It's great here, Dad," Nicky told him excitedly.

"If you're all settled, then I'm going to go," Evan said, and he felt Nicky hug him tight. "I love you."

Nicky gave him a squeeze. "I love you, too, Dad. Tell Clay I expect to see him for parents' day." Nicky leaned closer, and for a second Evan saw a shadow of the little boy he'd brought home. "Tell him 'I love you' for me."

"I will," Evan promised, stopping himself from kissing his son's forehead. "I have one last bit of good news for you, or at least for me," Evan said with a grin. "I found out today that the nuns retired."

"Dang, Dad," Nicky said with mock indignation. "No nun food," they said together, both of them laughing, with Nicky adding, "Send a care package anyway, just in case."

Nicky released him from the hug and stepped back, smiling before returning to his room, where the game and talking commenced almost immediately. Turning away, Evan walked out of the building and straight to his car. Driving down the hill, he followed the country road back to the highway. As he merged into traffic, he caught a glimpse of the school perched on its hill. Turning his attention back to the road, he drove toward home, leaving his past behind.

Evan spent much of the drive home thinking, his spirit lighter than he could ever remember feeling. The old demons seemed to have been vanquished. Granted, he tried not to let himself feel too elated, because whenever he did, something or someone would pull the rug from under him, but it was hard not to feel good. He'd faced his abuser and replaced the face that had tormented him for years with the image of the pitiable creature in the hospital bed. Rolling down the window, Evan let the sun-warmed air wash over him, breathing in and out deeply, expelling the last of the bad feelings, letting them fly away on the rush of air.

During the drive, Evan stopped for a light lunch before continuing home, pulling into the driveway in the late afternoon. He hadn't expected Clay to be home, so it wasn't a surprise when he didn't see his car in the driveway. He'd already tried calling a few times, but hadn't received an answer, which meant he was probably still taking care of things.

Walking into the house, Evan wandered upstairs to Nicky's room, which looked like Hurricane Nicolas had struck. Evan spent a while making the bed and picking up the dirty laundry, dumping it in the hamper in the bathroom, keeping himself busy. Finished with what he wanted to do, he closed the door. Walking across the hall, he had his hand on the doorknob when he heard a car horn honk from outside. Rushing outside, Evan saw Clay getting out of the car, closing the driver's door. "Did everything go okay?" Evan asked, hurrying toward the car, and he saw Clay grin.

"It just took a little longer than I expected, but it's done!" Clay told him energetically, pulling Evan into his arms for a hug before opening the back door.

Evan peered inside, and a huge pair of brown eyes peered back at him. "Hello, Anna," Evan said, reaching inside to remove the girl from her car seat. "Your big brother was sad he had to go on to school, but today it's official."

"Yes," Clay said from behind him. "Today, she's our daughter."

Evan lifted her out of the car, holding the eighteen-month-old in his arms before twirling in excited circles. Anna giggled and laughed. "You're really ours," Evan sang as he held her close.

"The judge terminated her mother's parental rights, as we expected, and signed the order of adoption. She's officially ours."

"Did her mother get any visitation?"

Clay bounced on his heels. "Nope. A life sentence for murder isn't conducive to being a proper parent, so the judge terminated all her rights. She's ours free and clear with no encumbrances or stipulations."

Evan stopped moving and rolled his eyes at Clay. "You're such a lawyer."

"And you love me," Clay shot back, leaning in for a kiss.

Evan gave him one on the lips while Anna raspberried Clay's cheek. "Let's get her inside. She probably needs a nap, considering we were in court or filing papers most of the day." Clay gave their little girl a kiss on the cheek. "She was very good," Clay said, tickling Anna's tummy. "Yes, you were."

Anna squirmed, and Evan set her down. She toddled a little, but then fell on her diapered butt. She got herself back up and took off across the lawn, falling again before getting to her feet once again. "Nic, Nic," she said, pointing toward the door and walking toward the front of the house. "Da Nic."

"Nicky's gone to school, Anna," Evan explained as he walked to her, scooping her into his arms. "I can't believe how far she's come in three months."

"Neither could the judge," Clay said, getting Anna's diaper bag out of the car. "She was absolutely amazed." When they'd first gotten Anna she was fifteen months old, malnourished, and unable to walk or talk. She'd taken her first steps from Evan to Nicky and never looked back. She'd started talking recently, and more words came every day.

"Dad," Anna said, pointing at Clay.

"Let's get you down for a nap, sweetheart," Evan said as Clay unlocked the door. Putting her down, she toddled through the house to the kitchen, patting on the refrigerator door. "I take it you're hungry," Clay commented, lifting her away before opening the door, handing her a piece of cheese he kept for her snacks. Flopping on the floor, she started eating right away—no preamble when it came to his girl and food. When she'd finished, Evan scooped her off the floor, carrying Anna upstairs to her room.

"Nic," Anna whined, pointing at Nicky's bedroom door as Evan stopped outside hers. Opening Nicky's door, he let her see that it was empty. "Nic," she cried, looking around the room, squirming to get down.

"Come on, Anna. Nicky's at school, but he'll be back. Let's get you down for a nap," Evan told her lightly as Anna kept looking around the room, tears rolling down her cheeks. "It's okay, sweet girl, he's not gone forever, and next month when we visit him, you can come too." Evan took her across the hall to her room, placing her on the changing table, where he changed her diaper and got her into a pair of pajamas, tears running down her cheeks the entire time.

Picking Anna up, he placed her against him before sticking his head out into the hall. "Clay, can you help me a second?" Evan called, and a few seconds later he heard Clay's footsteps on the stairs. "Would you bring me a phone and the number for St. Bart's. She's just not going to be consoled."

"Sure, hon," Clay said, pulling his cell out of his pocket. "I'll be right back," Clay added before returning with the phone number. Dialing, Evan waited until someone answered, walking and rocking Anna to try to calm her.

"Hello, I need to speak with Nicolas Donaldson, please." Evan waited and a few minutes later he heard Nicky's voice. "Nicky, there's someone who wants to speak with you," Evan told his son, and then he held the phone to Anna's ear. She quieted immediately, listening to the sound of Nicky's voice.

"Nic, Nic," she said excitedly, and then began to babble in her own language, talking to him like crazy.

"Okay, bye, Anna," he heard Nicky say.

"Bye," she said, and Evan took the phone away.

"She's been inconsolable since Clay brought her home and you weren't here," Evan explained. "I'm sorry to interrupt, but I also wanted to let you know that it's official, you have a baby sister." The whoop that came through the phone was nearly deafening.

"So everything went okay?" Nicky asked once he got over his celebrations.

"It seems to have. Clay hasn't told me all about it yet, but I'm sure he will. We'll all see you next month."

"Okay, Dad. Love you." Nicky hung up, and Evan disconnected the call while Anna yawned.

"Let's get you to bed," Evan told her, laying Anna in her crib. "I got your bunny for you." Evan handed her the same bunny Nicky had used. Evan had no idea why he'd kept it all those years, but once Anna arrived, she'd seen it and latched on to it tighter than anything else. "Night night," he added, giving her the bottle Clay had brought when he'd given him the phone number, then he left the room, seeing her eyes already closing.

In the hallway, Evan bumped into Clay and found himself being pulled into their bedroom. "So what happened at St. Bart's? Did you see Father Val?"

Evan sat on the edge of the bed, relating everything that had happened. When he was done, Clay whistled. "Sounds like your day was a lot more eventful than you planned."

"Yeah," Evan acknowledged, yawning himself. "I think I'll lie down for a while." Evan kicked off his shoes, lying on top of the bedspread. Clay covered him with a blanket before kicking off his own shoes and climbing on the bed behind him, spooning to Evan's back. "You know, I didn't think I wanted to see Brother Renier again for as long as I lived, but it was good. He can't hurt me or anyone anymore, ever."

"Did you forgive him?" Clay asked quietly.

"No. I thought about it, but what he did was unforgivable. Instead, I told him the truth, that there was a special place in hell waiting for him. He may not be able to hurt me anymore, but he deserves whatever justice gets meted out in the hereafter." Evan felt his eyes begin to drift closed.

"You've had nightmares about him for years," Clay told him, curling closer.

"I think those are over. He can't scare me now—the man looked like a skeleton with skin and eyes. There was nothing to him." Cradled in Clay's warm embrace, Evan let sleep take him.

"Da, da, da, da, da," Evan heard coming from Anna's room. Blinking his eyes open, he saw he'd been asleep for almost two hours. Clay still held him, and Evan didn't want to move, but Miss Leather Lungs definitely had other ideas.

"I'll go get her," Clay said with a yawn, slipping off the bed.

"Thanks. She's going to be hungry."

"Just like her dad, always hungry," Clay said quietly, leaning over the bed, and Evan twisted his head, getting a kiss while Clay patted his stomach.

173

"Are you trying to tell me I'm putting on weight?" Evan asked sheepishly.

"I wouldn't dream of it," Clay answered, the lips and hands slipping away as another round of calls from their daughter drifted into the room, this time definitely more urgent. "I'd better go before she starts throwing things."

Evan let his eyes drift closed, hearing Anna's calls turn to squeals of delight as Clay lifted her out of the crib, followed by Clay's low voice as he talked to Anna while he changed her. He didn't have to be there to see it. He knew from the sounds and because of Clay. Airplane noises got louder as Clay "flew" Anna into their bedroom, setting her on the bed next to him. "Da, Nic," she said into his ear, and Evan tugged her into a hug, lifting her little shirt before blowing bubbles on her belly to giggles of delight.

"She has a one-track mind, doesn't she?" Evan asked as he sat up, lifting Anna into the air. "Let's go get you fed and then your daddies have work to do." Evan was not above putting in a *Baby Einstein* DVD to keep Anna entertained so they could get things done around the house. He used the excuse that they were educational, but both he and Clay knew it was the one way to keep her occupied for half an hour. So, after putting Anna in her high chair and getting her fed, Evan put a DVD in the player and sat Anna in her chair so they could work for an hour to get ready for tomorrow as well as make dinner.

"The house seems so quiet without Nicky," Clay told Evan as they ate their own dinner, papers set aside on the table, both of them keeping an eye on Anna.

"I know," Evan replied, feeling sullen.

"It's okay to be sad, you know. He's growing up, and this is the first step in a progression that will result in him leaving home."

"Good grief, Clay. You sound like a lawyer more and more," Evan told his partner with a smirk.

"Sorry, but you know what I mean. Where God closes a door, He opens a window. You took Nicky to school today, his first step toward leaving home, the same day our adoption of Anna was finalized."

Evan fell silent, his mind mulling over what Clay had told him and how utterly true it was. Didn't mean he had to like it, though. Evan finished his dinner, but didn't get up from the table.

"What?" Clay asked when he found Evan staring at him.

"You're even more beautiful than when I met you in high school," Evan said, his fingers sliding through Clay's hair.

"I think we need to get our little princess bathed and in bed as soon as possible so I can have some alone time with her dad," Clay told him, eyes already darkening. Getting up, Clay put their dishes in the sink, returning to the table so he could lean over the back of Evan's chair, kissing him invitingly. "It's been too long," Clay whispered, hands sliding down Evan's chest, and Evan found himself involuntarily stretching into the touch with the added advantage of giving Clay more to touch.

"Da, Dad," Anna cried from the other room as she struggled to get out of the chair. If there was any loving to be had and she saw it, their little Anna had to be in the thick of it. Clay's hands slipped away, and after a nip at one of his ears, he heard Clay running into the other room, followed by the sounds of giggles and raspberries.

"I think it's time someone had her bath." Clay's happy voice rang through the house, followed by his footsteps on the stairs. Adding Anna to their family had been a bit of a trial, because neither of them had been around a baby before. Thankfully, their baby expert, Wendy, now the mother of two, had been on hand to guide them through those first few days. Getting up from the table,

Evan cleaned up the dishes as he heard bathwater being run. Once the water stopped, he heard more giggles and laughter filling the house. Finishing the dishes, Evan joined Clay in the bathroom.

"Da," Anna said, happily standing up in the tub so Evan could wrap her in the towel.

"Tomorrow, little girl, you and I get to go to school. I have to go to work, and you get to play with the other children in the daycare center," Evan said as he dried her. Clay was already cleaning up the bathroom while Evan took Anna into her room, getting a diaper on her before slipping her into her pajamas. As soon as he set her on the floor, Anna walked to her bookcase. "Boo," she said, pulling one from the case, carrying it to him. "Boo."

Taking the book, Evan sat in the chair, set Anna on his lap, giving her a bottle, and opened the cover. "Curious George…." Anna was nearly asleep when he finished the story. After taking the empty bottle away, he set her in her crib, knowing that she'd fall asleep quickly now. Covering her with a blanket, Evan placed her bunny next to her, quietly leaving the room.

Downstairs, he found the rooms dark and empty. Checking that he'd cleaned up everything in the kitchen, Evan went back upstairs, turning off the lights before walking into their bedroom. Clay lay on their bed, a pair of boxers on his still-slender hips. Cracking the door, Evan stripped out of his clothes before joining Clay on top of the covers. The light clicked off, plunging the room into darkness, but after more than a decade, light or no light, Evan knew his way intimately around the man lying next to him. He'd known him for what seemed like the best parts of his life, and for more than a decade, this man had been his lover.

Evan felt Clay's lips on his, gentle and sweet, the kiss quickly deepening as Evan felt the day slip away, his consciousness narrowing to only Clay. Even after all these years, all it took was a kiss from Clay to make his heart race and his blood heat. A lot of words weren't used; they weren't needed. The way Clay touched his cheek told him more than declarations of love that went on forever. Feeling Clay's tongue teasing his lip, Evan's lips parted, Clay's tongue dueling with his, fingers carding through Evan's hair, Clay's scent filling his nose.

Evan groaned softly as Clay's lips slipped away from his, and he tried to follow them, but Clay was too quick, and the groan morphed into a quiet moan as Clay's tongue slid along the skin of Evan's chest. "I know what you like, Ev. More than anyone in the world, I know what you like," Clay murmured against his damp skin, making him shiver slightly.

"I know you do," Evan answered softly as his shorts slid down his hips, and he squirmed under Clay before flicking them away with his foot. Arms and hands slipped around his waist as Evan felt Clay's warm fingers around his erection, hips bucking slightly at the sensation.

Clay's chuckling laugh filled the room before he kissed a trail across Evan's skin, nipples, stomach, belly button— all passed under those searing lips, and then Clay's hot tongue slid over him. With a hiss, Evan bucked, wanting more. The chuckle deepened, and Evan thought for a second this was going to be one of those times when Clay teased him to complete and utter distraction. But then Clay took him into his hot mouth, and the breath whooshed from Evan's lungs. Nothing in the world felt as good as Clay's talented mouth, unless it was being inside Clay's body. "Clay," Evan moaned, trying to keep from being loud when he wanted to shout.

Evan bucked slightly, and Clay met each and every movement, sucking him deep until Evan thought his head would never stop throbbing. A finger joined his cock, teasing along his skin before slipping away, pressing lightly to his entrance before sliding into his body, the digit sliding along that spot, and he jumped slightly, pressing himself deep into Clay's mouth. "Like I said, I know what you like," Clay reiterated before taking him deep, sucking him hard. Evan didn't know which way to turn and that was probably what Clay had in mind.

"I'm not gonna last," Evan said, and he felt Clay's lips slip away.

"That's the idea," Clay told him, voice deep and resonant in the dark room. Then the lips returned and Evan was gone, flying high on the wings of passion Clay provided as he came hard, Clay's throat milking him dry.

Evan gasped for breath as his body gave out, collapsing back against the mattress. He could still feel Clay's finger inside his body until it, too, slipped away. Lying next to him, underwear now gone, he felt Clay's hand on his stomach, tugging him close. Lying on his side, he felt Clay's erection slide between his cheeks, and slowly, carefully, join them together. Not being as young as he used to be, it took a few minutes for his body to catch up with his own desire, but Clay's magic hands soon had him raring to go, and it wasn't long before Clay's own soft gasps and whimpers were joined by Evan's renewed vigor. "Love you, Clay," Evan whimpered, eyes clamped shut as he came for the second time, feeling Clay still and throb inside him.

Spent, satiated, and as happy as he could ever remember being, Evan curled close to his lover once he returned from the bathroom, holding him close, lost in his own thoughts and Clay's warmth. "What are you thinking about?" Clay asked.

"Something you said earlier about God opening a window." Evan turned over to face Clay, fingers stroking his rough cheek. "You're my window, you know that?" Evan felt Clay shake his head. "Well, you are, and you've always been. Through most of the tragedies and hardships in my life you've been there. At times, doors may have closed for me, but you've always been my window," Evan said softly, kissing Clay with all the feeling he could muster.

ANDREW GREY grew up in western Michigan with a father who loved to tell stories and a mother who loved to read them. Since then he has lived throughout the country and traveled throughout the world. He has a master's degree from the University of Wisconsin-Milwaukee and works in information systems for a large corporation. Andrew's hobbies include collecting antiques, gardening, and leaving his dirty dishes anywhere but in the sink (particularly when writing). He considers himself blessed with an accepting family, fantastic friends, and the world's most supportive and loving partner. Andrew currently lives in beautiful historic Carlisle, Pennsylvania.

Visit Andrew's web site at http://www.andrewgreybooks.com and blog at http://andrewgreybooks.livejournal.com/. E-mail him at andrewgrey@comcast.net.

Contemporary Romance by ANDREW GREY

http://www.dreamspinnerpress.com

Contemporary Romance by ANDREW GREY

http://www.dreamspinnerpress.com

Also by ANDREW GREY

http://www.dreamspinnerpress.com

Contemporary Romance by ANDREW GREY

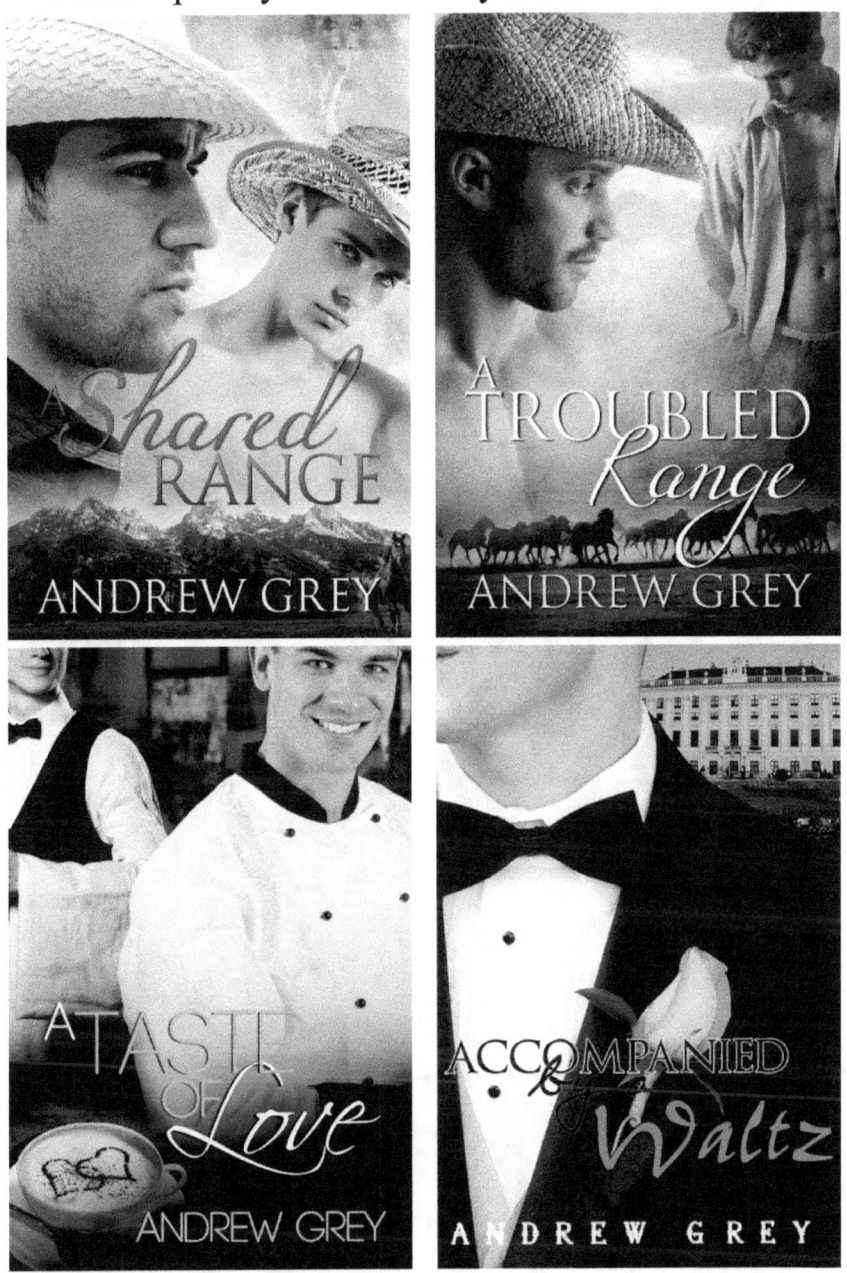

Contemporary Fantasy by ANDREW GREY